BY PEARL S. BUCK

Fiction

EAST WIND: WEST WIND, 1930
THE GOOD EARTH, 1931
SONS, 1932
THE FIRST WIFE AND OTHER STORIES, 1933
THE MOTHER, 1934
A HOUSE DIVIDED, 1935
HOUSE OF EARTH [*trilogy of* The Good Earth, *revised*, Sons *and* A House Divided], 1935
THIS PROUD HEART, 1938
THE PATRIOT, 1939
OTHER GODS, 1941
TODAY AND FOREVER, 1941
DRAGON SEED, 1942
THE PROMISE, 1943
PORTRAIT OF A MARRIAGE, 1945
THE TOWNSMAN [as John Sedges], 1945
PAVILION OF WOMEN, 1946
THE ANGRY WIFE [as John Sedges], 1947
FAR AND NEAR: STORIES OF JAPAN, CHINA, AND AMERICA, 1947
PEONY, 1948
KINFOLK, 1949

THE LONG LOVE [as John Sedges], 1949
GOD'S MEN, 1951
BRIGHT PROCESSION [as John Sedges], 1952
THE HIDDEN FLOWER, 1952
VOICES IN THE HOUSE [as John Sedges], 1953
COME, MY BELOVED, 1953
IMPERIAL WOMAN, 1956
LETTER FROM PEKING, 1957
COMMAND THE MORNING, 1959
FOURTEEN STORIES, 1961
A BRIDGE FOR PASSING, 1962
THE LIVING REED, 1963
DEATH IN THE CASTLE, 1965
THE TIME IS NOON, 1967
THE NEW YEAR, 1968
THE GOOD DEED, 1969
THE THREE DAUGHTERS OF MADAME LIANG, 1969
MANDALA, 1970
THE GODDESS ABIDES, 1972
ALL UNDER HEAVEN, 1973
THE RAINBOW, 1974
EAST AND WEST, 1975
SECRETS OF THE HEART, 1976
THE LOVERS AND OTHER STORIES, 1977

Translation

ALL MEN ARE BROTHERS [SHUI HU CHUAN], 1933

General

IS THERE A CASE FOR FOREIGN MISSIONS? [*pamphlet*], 1932

THE EXILE, 1936
FIGHTING ANGEL, 1936
THE CHINESE NOVEL, 1939

OF MEN AND WOMEN, 1941
AMERICAN UNITY AND ASIA, 1942
WHAT AMERICA MEANS TO ME, 1943
THE SPIRIT AND THE FLESH [*combining* The Exile *and* Fighting Angel],1944
TALK ABOUT RUSSIA, with Masha Scott, 1945
TELL THE PEOPLE, 1945
HOW IT HAPPENS: TALK ABOUT THE GERMAN PEOPLE, 1914-1933, with Erna von Pustau, 1947
AMERICAN ARGUMENT, with Eslanda Goode Robeson, 1949
THE CHILD WHO NEVER GREW, 1950
MY SEVERAL WORLDS, 1954
FRIEND TO FRIEND, with Carlos P. Romulo, 1958
THE JOY OF CHILDREN, 1964

CHILDREN FOR ADOPTION, 1965
THE GIFTS THEY BRING, with Gweneth T. Zarfoss, 1965
FOR SPACIOUS SKIES: JOURNEY IN DIALOGUE, with Theodore F. Harris, 1966
TO MY DAUGHTERS, WITH LOVE, 1967
CHINA AS I SEE IT, 1970
THE KENNEDY WOMEN, 1970
THE STORY BIBLE, 1971
CHINA: PAST AND PRESENT, 1972
A COMMUNITY SUCCESS STORY, with Elisabeth Waechter, 1972
ONCE UPON A CHRISTMAS, 1972
PEARL BUCK'S ORIENTAL COOKBOOK, 1972
WORDS OF LOVE, 1974

· Juvenile

THE YOUNG REVOLUTIONIST, 1932
STORIES FOR LITTLE CHILDREN, 1940
THE CHINESE CHILDREN NEXT DOOR, 1942
THE WATER-BUFFALO CHILDREN, 1943
THE DRAGON FISH, 1944
YU LAN: FLYING BOY OF CHINA, 1945
THE BIG WAVE, 1948
ONE BRIGHT DAY, 1950
THE MAN WHO CHANGED CHINA: THE STORY OF SUN YAT-SEN, 1953
JOHNNY JACK AND HIS BEGINNINGS, 1954

THE BEECH TREE, 1955
CHRISTMAS MINIATURE, 1957
MY SEVERAL WORLDS [Abridged for Younger Readers], 1957
THE CHRISTMAS GHOST, 1960
WELCOME CHILD, 1964
THE BIG FIGHT, 1965
THE LITTLE FOX IN THE MIDDLE, 1966
MATTHEW, MARK, LUKE AND JOHN, 1967
THE CHINESE STORY TELLER, 1971
A GIFT FOR THE CHILDREN, 1973
MRS. STARLING'S PROBLEM, 1973

The Lovers
and other stories

Pearl S. Buck
THE LOVERS
and other stories
The John Day Company   New York

Designed by Joy Chu

Manufactured in the United States of America

Library of Congress Cataloging in Publication Data

Buck, Pearl Sydenstricker, 1892-1973.
The lovers and other stories.

CONTENTS: Answer to life.—The two women.—Miranda.—
The kiss. [etc.]
I. Title.
PZ3.B8555Lr   [PS3503.U198]   813'.5'2   76-56819
ISBN 0-381-97109-0

10   9   8   7   6   5   4   3   2   1

Contents

Answer to Life

I

JENNET MACLEAN, rising from among the dark-robed seniors of her college graduating class, searched the rows of seats in front of her. She had watched for an hour every stir in the audience. Would her mother be there to hear her? They had faced the possible disappointment this morning at breakfast. The telephone rang and her mother reached for the receiver without rising from her chair. Jennet had watched her mother's face take on its grave concentrated look, "your medical look," Jennet always called it. She listened to the one-sided conversation.

"Have you taken the child's temperature? . . . Then wrap him in blankets. I'll be there in half an hour. No, don't feed him anything."

Her mother put up the receiver without telling who it was. She never spoke of her patients even in the family. To any casual eye she went on exactly as she had been, but Jennet, knowing every change in that worn face and small erect figure, saw the slight tightening of nerve and muscle. She had not been able to keep from crying out.

"Oh, Mother, I hope you won't miss my Commencement!"

"I shan't," Dr. Angie Maclean said. She threw an incisive blue glance at her tall dark daughter. Jennet looked like her father, and Dr. Maclean was endlessly thankful for that. "It's been a handicap to me to be small and light," she often thought. "Not that I want Jennet's life to be like mine," she always added.

Her eyes turned to her husband sitting at the head of the table and all the incision faded from them. He sat tall and dignified, his dark eyes vague, his lips kind.

"You'll go with Jennet, won't you, Gareth?"

Gareth Maclean hesitated the inevitable instant necessary before he said anything.

"Certainly, Angie." He looked up at her when he pronounced her name, and she saw as she had seen thousands of times in these years the faint blankness of his look, the incomprehensible blankness which she never mentioned to anybody, even to Jennet. Did Jennet notice? No, it was not likely. Jennet had been a year old when Gareth came back from France and she remembered him only as he had been ever since.

"That will be nice, darling," she said gently. She smiled at them both, and with her unconsciously curt little nod in a moment she had left the room.

Down in the front pews of the college chapel Jennet now saw her father. He had sat motionless through the long exercise, his handsome white head drooping a little, his thin hands folded. She knew those hands perfectly for hers were exactly like them. "Surgeon's hands," her mother had once said in her soft abrupt voice. She had taken one of Jennet's young hands and examined it. "Like your father's," she had said and put it down again.

Gareth at this moment lifted his head and saw his

daughter standing tall above him in her long black gown. He smiled at her uncertainly and when she smiled back at him he felt suddenly happy. Jennet was a lovely girl. She did everything well—a comfort, of course, to Angie. He sighed and his head dropped again. Jennet's voice floated out, very clear, above him somewhere.

"We who are now to begin our life in the world . . ." No, her mother was not here, she was thinking. Well, then, she must go on exactly as though she were. Then at this moment the chapel door opened and she saw her mother's small slender figure enter, march down the aisle halfway, and without self-consciousness she waved her hand, sat down, and took off her hat. Jennet breathed deeply and lifted her head high and began again. "We who are now to begin our life in the world," she repeated confidently.

"Oh, but I was afraid you wouldn't be there," she murmured, squeezing her mother's little soft body. "And I'd never have forgiven you!"

They were at home again and in her room. Upon the bed lay a jumble of robe and mortar board, flowers, graduation presents and diploma not yet opened.

"I only just made it," Angie Maclean gasped. Her daughter's strong young arms crushed her ribs but for nothing would she have mentioned it. Gareth used to hug her like that in the old days when they were at Johns Hopkins together.

"Now," Jennet commanded her happily, "sit

down in my big chair like that, and fold your little hands like that, and wait until I show you—'' She put her mother into the red armchair and folded one hand on the other, and then plucked the diploma out of the pile on the bed. ''Now, I untie it,'' she chanted, ''and now I unroll it, and now I show it to you. For four years, Dr. Maclean, I've slaved for this—oh, Mother!'' Jennet sat down suddenly on a footstool. ''They've given me a summa cum laude!''

''Why not?'' Her mother's voice was calm, but her eyes began to shine.

''Oh, I didn't expect it!''

''Phi Beta Kappa and all?''

''No! Why, somebody said the dean said all of the summas were men—as usual!''

''Not necessarily as usual,'' her mother said.

Jennet laughed. ''Nevertheless, Dr. Maclean, the fact remains it *is* unusual, for your daughter, at least.''

''Not at all,'' her mother repeated. Then she put to Jennet the question she had never put all these years, not wanting to influence her one way or another, not knowing herself how in the furthest secrets of her own heart she wanted Jennet to answer. ''And what will you do with it?''

Jennet's dark eyebrows flew. ''This?''

''This!'' her mother said steadily.

''Why, go on to medical, of course!''

So, Dr. Maclean thought, her heart ought now to be at rest. Jennet had decided absolutely for herself. She had seen for herself what it was to be a doctor—no, more, a woman doctor. She had neither hidden her own hardships nor complained of them, except that one, most secret, which had nothing to do with her professional life.

"You're quite sure?"

"Yes!"

One of Jennet's charms was the way she cried "Yes!", full, happy, onrushing. Still, if she could be half as sure as Jennet, as sure as she would have been had Jennet been a boy—the John she had always wanted and never had, simply because she couldn't, Gareth having come back to her as he did! There had been no time when she could have stopped to have another child of her own. It had taken all her strength—

"You won't find it easy," she said.

"I don't care," Jennet said. She smiled at her mother robustly and began very carefully to roll up the diploma.

"Specialty?" her mother asked.

Jennet dropped the diploma and held up her hands. "Surgery," she said.

"That," her mother said gravely, "will be the hardest of all."

Those fearless dark eyes, so like Gareth's when she first knew him!

"Surgery has been peculiary a man's field," she said quietly.

"As if that mattered—now!" Jennet laughed. Her rich gay laughter rolled out of her throat. Everything in this girl was big, her mother thought watching her, this big laughter, the beautiful big thin hands, the tall body and the noble head. But how feminine it all was, the mouth how tender and the softly curling dark hair, how childlike!

"I never before wished you were a boy," she said suddenly.

"Do you now?" Jennet grew grave.

"Somehow, I do."

"Why now?"

"So that you could start even."

Mother and daughter, they looked at each other.

"Are you brave enough for an almost hopeless handicap, Jennet?"

"As a woman, Moms?"

"As a woman."

Jennet pushed back her black hair. Then she gave her big full-throated cry, "Yes!"

"It's her eternal answer to life," her mother thought, and held her peace.

"Why choose surgery, Jennet?"

In the office of the dean of the College of Surgery, Jennet sat across the desk from Dr. Farland, whom she had known all her life.

"It's what I want to do, sir."

"There are so many other jobs easier."

Jennet's sweet mouth curved. "Did you think of that when you were my age?"

"I wasn't a woman," Dr. Farland said bluntly. He passed his hand over his eyes. Was he tired or only needing glasses at last?

"That's nonsense." Jennet's clear voice annoyed him unaccountably.

"Theoretically, yes. Practically, no. Surgeons are mostly men and all too human. Besides—" He looked at his watch. Half an hour and he must be in the operating room! He shuffled Jennet's papers together. "It's only commonsense to face what is. Why not go into children's diseases or women's work? You'd have no trouble there."

"Because I want to be a surgeon," Jennet said.

He lost his patience, always fragile nowadays. He knew why, too. It was folly to care because his only son did not want to be a doctor. But he did care. He himself was the fifth generation in his family of doctors. For Francis so lightly to refuse even to discover whether or not he might be mistaken in his decision, to refuse even one year of medical study, was to break faith with those generations of five doctors in his ancestry. And his mother took the boy's part. If Edith had known how nearly she had lost all that she valued in life, her stable position as his wife, her comfortable income—though of course he would never have let her suffer—and now, after their sharp discussion last night when Francis had refused him, to have this girl come into his office and want to be what his own son could not! "Well, I won't take you in surgery," he said sharply. "There's no relying on women students. I've tried before. We spend time and strength on them and in a year or two they marry and it's all wasted.'' He rose. ''I've got to go.''

She rose too. ''You'll have to take me.''

''Aren't you going to get married?''

''That has nothing to do with my being a surgeon, I think, Dr. Farland.''

''A surgeon can't call his time his own.''

''All right,'' she said, ''I won't call my time my own.''

''A surgeon's nerves have got to be hard.''

''Mine are,'' she said.

''Women—'' he said unwillingly, ''you're constitutionally unfitted for the sort of thing a surgeon has to do.''

''Try me!'' she said.

''Damn you,'' he said ruefully, ''I remember you were a stubborn child and now you've grown up into a stubborn woman—'' But he laughed suddenly and scrawled his name across a blank line. ''All right!'' he shouted from the door. ''Watch me make you sweat, young woman!''

''Swell!'' she cried.

Dr. Farland paused.

''How's your father?''

''He's splendid,'' she said, smiling. ''He's always well.''

''Wish he'd come up here and operate sometimes,'' Dr. Farland grumbled. ''He knows more about cutting up hearts than anybody else does. If you're half as good a surgeon, I'll eat crow for what I've said to you today.'' He hurried on.

"Get ready for crow, then,'' she called after him. She went back into the empty office and collected her papers, her mouth still smiling. Of course she would have her way, she thought gaily. She always did. That was because she knew what she wanted. When you knew what you wanted, you simply pursued your way to it. And she knew and had known for years that she wanted to be a surgeon—not fussing with ills and medicines, but cutting evil away, swift and clean, out of human bodies. Slipping her papers into a too-full envelope, her eyes fell on a silver-framed picture on the desk. Francis! She had not seen him for a year. She picked up the big picture in both hands and looked at it. Somehow or other she and Francis had missed each other at vacations this whole year, and last summer he had travelled.

She studied the handsome young face. She and Francis had played together when they were little, but school had separated them. He had gone to Groton and she had stayed home and gone to a girls' school. And then as they grew up the distance between them had not grown less. Francis had never asked her to a dance—never, indeed, asked her for anything.

She set the photograph down again. From that lower level his eyes seemed turned upward to gaze at her. It was the same shy, doubting look he had had as a little boy. He had been a sensitive little boy, and yet a wilful one. He always tried to snatch her toys, and yet there were times when she was happier with him than she had ever been with anyone else.

"It would be fun to know what he's really like," she thought. But in a moment she had forgotten him. She was hurrying home to her mother, to tell her.

"Mother!" she shouted loudly at the front door. So she had shouted always from the time she was a little girl. If her mother were home, she would hear her call back where she was. But often there was no answer.

There was none today. She pulled off her hat and flung it on the hall table. Then through the open door of the library she saw her father, his head bent over a book.

"Hello, Dad," she called.

He lifted his eyes. "Hello, dear," he said.

She went to him and leaned on his shoulder. "Trollope," she observed. "Haven't you read everything Trollope ever wrote by now?"

"Many times," he said. He laid his head back and looked up at her, smiling, and she saw with an instant's start how strange his face looked in the unusual position, how young underneath its age.

"Then why?" she asked.

"Oh, habit, maybe," he acknowledged, "a certain pleasantness in knowing exactly what's going to happen."

"I'd hate that." She moved away so she could see him properly again. "Where's Mother?"

He looked at his wristwatch. "Early for her to be back, isn't it?"

"Maybe it is." She lingered a moment, too restless to sit down. Then she had to tell someone. "Dad, I signed up for surgery this morning."

"Did you, Jennet?" Her father's eyes, stealing toward his book, peered and lifted to hers.

"Dr. Farland didn't think much of it."

"No?" His voice was almost polite.

"What do you think of it, Dad?"

"I?" He hesitated. "I don't know, Jennet."

"But Dad, you're a surgeon, too!"

His eyes grew troubled. "Yes, I know."

She pressed him. "Dr. Farland says you know more about heart surgery than anybody he knows."

"Yes," her father said, hesitating again. "Well, I specialized in that."

"Why did you give it up, Dad?"

"I? Well—" he paused and looked about the room. "I haven't exactly given it up."

"You don't operate very often."

"No," he agreed, "no, not very often." He frowned, concentrating. "The last operation I did was about a year ago. Farland asked me to stand in on it. Then suddenly in the middle of what he was doing he was taken ill. He felt faint, I remember. So I finished it for him."

"That was Mrs. Kingston, wasn't it?"

"Yes, Mrs. Kingston."

"I saw her yesterday as well as ever."

"Yes, I believe she recovered."

Never had her father been more hesitating. She looked at him closely. He wet his lips and turned his head away from her.

"Dad, are you ill?"

"I? No—no, of course not."

He sat looking away from her, agony in his eyes.

"But you look so strange!"

She was alarmed and she went toward him impetuously and to her horror saw him shrink away from her. He actually put up his hand against her. She stopped, staring at him. Then his hand dropped and he turned his head away again. In that instant she saw him as she never had. This vague, kindly, handsome, white-haired man who moved so gently about the house, who spoke so little and went out so seldom—was there something wrong with her father?

Before she could consider the answer to her question she heard her mother's light step at the door, her mother's clear voice.

"Why, darlings! Gareth, what's the matter?"

"I?" His eyes turned to her. "Nothing, Angie."

"No?" She went to him quickly and touched his forehead and his hands. "Your hands are very cold. Have you been out for a walk today, Gareth?"

"I? No—no, I haven't. I've been reading."

"Come then, we'll take a little walk, you and I."

He waited a moment, then closed his book carefully on the marker and rose. "That will be pleasant, Angie." He smiled down at her, a tall, strong-looking man in his middle fifties. His look grew concerned for her. "But you must have more on than that thin thing."

"Yes," she said, "you are right, of course, Gareth—very right and wise."

Why, Jennet thought, watching them, did her mother give hearty praise for so small a thing? Besides the day was warm. Her heart quivered. Was there something going on before her eyes which she had never seen?

"Will you come, too, Jennet?" her mother asked.

"No thanks, Mother," she replied. Then she remembered her news. "Mother, I've signed up."

Her mother's gaze, brooding upon her father, moved reluctantly to her.

"Signed up, dear child?"

"For surgery, Mother!" Could her mother really have forgotten the most important thing in the world?

"Oh—of course, dear!"

No of course about it, Jennet thought, receiving her mother's quick kiss.

"You'd forgotten," she said loudly.

Her mother laughed, shamefacedly. "You know your mother! I forget anything when I'm working. So will you, rapscallion! Someday you'll forget I'm alive. But I won't scold you. I'll understand."

"So do I," Jennet said swiftly. "I never blame you for anything, Mother." Then she made herself smile. "Run along, you two, by yourselves," she said, "you don't want me anyway."

She went with them to the door though, and kissed them both warmly, and then stood looking after them.

Her father was a head above her mother's little figure. No one, she thought, seeing that small dark-robed woman clinging to the tall erect man, would dream that there was one of New York's most famous doctors. Yes, her mother was now that, a diagnostician so sensitive and so exact that people came from far and near merely to have Dr. Angie Maclean tell them what was wrong with them.

"She would know if anything were wrong with Dad," Jennet thought. "And she would have told me, wouldn't she?"

Why not? She and her mother had always told each other everything. She was so young that upon this easy notion her mind was instantly at rest. She ran upstairs to her room, full of pleasure because she was to have her own way. She was going to be a surgeon. Upon that bedrock of decision she suddenly felt everything rise and grow gay. She was going to be a surgeon but meanwhile college was over and there was the summer and she was going to play and have fun and do as she liked and then next autumn work as no one had ever worked. Brain surgery, maybe, or heart, the hardest, most delicate, most difficult, that was what she wanted to do—tops, anyway, whatever she did.

The small clock in her room struck four. She was finding the day a little long. This first day free of school and work. There was plenty to do. There were plenty of people to call up to tell she was home. But somehow she had not done anything or called up anyone. She did not know what she wanted to do first. In spite of her determination to play and have a good time, the knowledge that she had this morning definitely committed herself to an enormous task sobered her thoughts. Four o'clock —now if her mother's office hours could be over. She could talk everything over with her mother and perhaps then her mind would be free.

At this moment she heard a man's voice downstairs. The door of her room was open and she tiptoed out and looked down the stairwell, upon a smoothly parted blonde head. Essie the maid was saying, "I don't know where Miss Jennet is, sir. I haven't seen her come in. Still," she hesitated, "there's her hat."

Jennet leaned over the rail. "Here I am," she said. Her voice floated downward like the note of a bell and the young man lifted his face. She saw who it was. "Hello, Francis Farland," she said, "what have you come for?"

"To see you," he said, laughing. "You're just as impolite as you used to be!"

"No, I'm not. I'm lots nicer!" She heard her voice dropping down like the note of a bell again.

"Come and let me see for myself," he said, and his voice seemed to climb up to her. It was a pleasant voice, light and tenor in its quality, but a man's voice.

"In a minute," she said. In that minute she brushed her hair hard and curled the ends up and powdered her nose, and then, frowning at the severity of her white linen suit, she took it off and put on a soft green dress with a ruffle for a collar and then brushed her hair again. In the mirror she looked at herself and laughed. "What's the matter with me?" she thought. "It's only Francis!"

She refused to look at herself again and went downstairs slowly, not caring, she thought, whether she saw him or not. He was standing in the living room, his hands in his pockets, waiting for her, his blue eyes cool.

"But he's enormously improved," she thought, and put out her hand. "Hello, you," she said.

"Hello, yourself," he replied.

But still she was just a little taller than he.

"How you've grown," he said mischievously.

"Shut up," she said pleasantly. "Anyway, so have you."

"My best isn't as good as yours." He dropped into a chair and took out a cigarette. "Smoke?"

"No, thanks."

"You ought to—it would stunt you a little."

She stared at him. "I thought you had changed but you haven't. You still like to pull my hair!"

He laughed. "Oh, well! You're still a girl!"

She waited, examining him frankly. He looked amazingly like the boy she had known, she decided. He was as blonde, a little less pretty and a little more handsome, but his mouth was still wilful. The hand that held the cigarette was well shaped, but it trembled a little. Was he shy?

"Are you glad you've finished college?" she asked.

"I'll say I am," he replied. "Gosh, I just squeaked through, though."

She did not answer this.

"I suppose you took all the keys and buttons and knickknacks?" he asked. His blue eyes moved lazily to her face. A damned good-looking girl, he was thinking, but too big.

"Oh, maybe," she said. Some instinct made her hide the truth and then she despised her own instinct. Why should she pretend she was brainless? But she was saved the necessity for honesty. The door opened and her mother came in from her office and there were the commonplaces of talk between two different generations. She was silent, listening to the courteous inquiries of the elder to the younger. She listened and learned that Francis was home for the summer. No, he didn't know what he wanted to do. He was going to look around. Maybe he would find an opening somewhere in an office. He'd always thought he'd like to go into real estate. Anyway, something not too hard on the brain, he said laughing.

"You're not following your father, then," Dr. Maclean said.

"Gosh, no," Francis said gaily. "We've rowed that out to a finish. I want a little life of my own. Luckily mother agrees with me." He rose and crushed out his second cigarette and glanced at his wristwatch. "Well, I must be going—got to meet someone for lunch." He turned to Jennet. "Busy all the time?"

"Not quite," she smiled at him.

"Want to dance somewhere?"

"I think so—time and place being right."

"Tomorrow—at the Roundhouse?"

"Right."

They nodded, and she caught her mother's eyes watching her gravely.

It was midnight and Jennet had just come in. Her mother was in her office. In the hall she saw the light under the door and she opened it, softly. But her mother was not at her desk. She was in the laboratory beyond, studying a slide upon a microscope, her face hidden by an eyeshield. Jennet crossed the office on tiptoe.

"You didn't wait up for me, Mother?"

"No, dear child." Her mother pulled off the shield. The strong silver light under the microscope flared upward against her face. "Did you have a good time?"

"It was fun—though we didn't do much." Jennet hesitated a moment, searching for more to tell her mother. "We just danced and had a drink and danced some more. Francis saw some people he knew, sort of silly people, but it didn't matter. Anyway, we were all just silly and that was fun. It's the first thing I've had that's made me realize college is over and this is vacation."

"What sort of boy is Francis now? I ought to say man, not boy."

Jennet hesitated again. "Still a good deal of a boy,

Mother. He's rather sweet, though charming, I suppose. He knows how to do the right things for a girl.''

"Such as?''

Jennet laughed. She went to her mother, towering over her. "Oh, I don't know! But he makes me feel little and pretty—me, a big gawk!'' She ruffled her mother's untidy hair.

"Would you like to be little and pretty?''

"I'd like to be like you!'' She kissed the top of her mother's head.

"My smallness has been a great disadvantage to me,'' her mother said solemnly. "Nobody ever believed I could do anything.''

"Always a disadvantage?'' Jennet demanded teasingly. "Even when you were a girl? Even when you and Dad first knew each other?''

How did the child think of that, Dr. Maclean asked herself. No, it had been no disadvantage to be a little thing that day she had first met Gareth, a tall young student surgeon. She had never been pretty, or at least so she had thought, though she had had little enough time to think of such things since she was born into a country doctor's household. But Gareth had made her feel pretty that day, even in a laboratory, even in her crumpled white uniform.

"Why, you tiny little thing!'' he had said suddenly. "What are you?''

"I'm a student, too,'' she had said severely. "I'm going to be a doctor.''

"I don't believe it,'' he had said. "You're some

sort of a little bird, a human hummingbird, maybe.''

"I'm to specialize in children's diseases."

"Being a baby yourself," he had said, and laughed. Then he had stared at her. "You're pretty," he said softly, and then had added, "anything as little as you is always pretty."

"Don't answer my impudence," Jennet said suddenly. "Forget it, little 'un."

"No," her mother said fondly.

She gave her mother one of her enormous squeezing hugs. "Well, then!" she cried. But she did not notice that her mother said nothing at all to that.

She went upstairs, undressed, bathed and put on fresh pajamas and brushed her hair. She ought to be sleepy, but she was not, she thought, looking at her bed. She turned away from it and sat down on the window seat, put out the light and looked out over the city, a maze of lights beneath her window. The Roundhouse was a silly place, but she had really had a good time, though why, she could not think. Yes, she could. It was fun to be with Francis, sheer fun. He had made her feel the way she used to feel sometimes when she was a little girl, that with nobody in the world could she have as good a time as with him. Why?

"I'm just in a state, that's all," she thought. "He's the first man." She tried to be cynical. This city was full of good-looking men. The world was full of them. Next autumn in the College of Surgery there would be hundreds of them. Certainly she was not going to think Francis the only one.

*   *   *

''Know why I came to see you?'' he had said. His eyes were really on a level with her when they danced together, or so very nearly. She had swayed backward a little to look into the pleasant mischievous blue eyes.

''I can't imagine,'' she said.

''Dad said that you had come into his office. But that wasn't why.''

''No?''

''He said you wanted to be a surgeon. Then he looked at me. I could tell what he was thinking. 'What's the world coming to when the women want to do the real work?' That's what he was thinking and wanting to say to me and didn't dare. Mother would have started another argument. She's very feminine and all that. She doesn't believe in women outside the home. Neither do I.''

She laughed at him. ''That has nothing to do with me!'' But she pulled away from him a little.

He drew her back. ''That wasn't why I came to see you, stupid! Want to know why?''

''Not much.''

He laughed at her now. ''You do want to know— much! It was because Dad said you'd grown into a damned beautiful girl and it was a waste of time for you to think about surgery.'' His arm had tightened about her and she had not answered. The music was soft and slow, and they danced together in complete rhythm.

Then after a moment she said very distinctly, "I'd never be happy if I didn't do all I want to do."

"Stay beautiful!" he had whispered.

The music stopped as he spoke. Their arms dropped, and they went back to their table. And the next moment he had seen his friends and called to them to come over to their table. And that was all.

Was she a beautiful woman? She knew her face and did not know it. Now it seemed to her fearfully important if someone thought she was—if *he* thought she was. She rose and walked across the floor two or three times, her hands in her curly hair.

Downstairs in the library Dr. Angie Maclean heard that tigerish young tread back and forth above her head. She was sipping a glass of milk as she often did when she worked late. She finished the glass and took it to the kitchen and rinsed it in cold water and set it on the sink. Then she took a quick look about the kitchen. Everything was neat. This English woman she now had was clean, though she would never be able to make coffee. She must get one of those foolproof electric things when she had time—maybe Jennet could get it for her.

She prowled about, feeling a sort of homesickness as she did so. In those sweet old days when she and Gareth were young she had done all her own work. Yes, all the skill of laboratory technique so conscientiously and thoroughly acquired she had applied to the small kitchen of their first home. After all that training and her internship she had given up what she had thought of as her work, to be Gareth's wife. It had not been sudden. She had finished her training doggedly, determined to have it before she made her mind up about marriage— no, not about marriage, but about Gareth. She had loved Gareth so wholly that Gareth alone was what decided her. She wanted Gareth only to be her work, Gareth and his home and his children.

"I have no right to ask you to marry me." So he had proposed to her at last when they had been in love with each other for two years. "I don't want you to marry me," he had gone on abruptly. "I don't believe in doctors marrying each other. It never works."

"I know it," she had said.

"But I can't marry anyone else," he had said furiously, "because I can't stop loving you."

"I'm glad of that," she had said.

He had lifted her into his arms then and squeezed the breath out of her body until she had grown faint, and then he had been frightened until she felt able to laugh, in a minute or two.

"Don't worry about marrying a doctor," she had gasped.

He had stared at her until she went on to explain.

"I'm going to be your wife and not a doctor."

"Sure you want to?" he had asked gravely.

"I'm very sure," she had answered.

He had never spoken of it again, nor had she. Nor, indeed, had anyone. Everybody took it for granted that the woman gave up everything in marriage. She sighed, staring down into a drawer full of shining pot lids. Of course it would not have been giving up anything, perhaps, if Gareth had not gone to France—and come back again. She closed the drawer and put out the lights and went upstairs.

At Jennet's door she paused. Still that young stride, padding across the floor! She paused, put out her hand to the door and then drew it back. She would not enter. What she had done—or not done—must be no law for Jennet's life. There was nothing new about love, but the young could not know it. She went on down the hall, her heart aching in her breast, but she had grown used to that and paid no attention to it, or very little. It had been valuable in its way, this perpetual heartache. It had helped her to diagnose in other women those symptoms of too early whitening hair and the drying out of color and freshness from the skin. Part of her skill was her cleverness in discovering the emotional causes of illness.

She opened the door of her room and switched on the light. The door was open into Gareth's room, but his room was dark. She tiptoed into it and to his bed. Then in the light from her room she could see his face. He was deeply asleep, as though he had been asleep for hours, and he did not stir. This, too, he had done all those years since he came back. He had gone early to bed every night except the few nights a year they went out to theater or dinner, and always he fell into this deep and deathly sleep. It was late in the morning before he woke, sometimes even long after she had breakfasted and gone to work. A few times a month they breakfasted together.

And he never woke in the night. It was almost impossible to wake him. She stood, studying him, the old anxious fears pulling at her. Had she done well to hide the truth from everyone? But to whom could she have gone? Time and again she had had him tested for any physical cause for his change. She had made tests herself until he had refused more. Physically he was in perfect health. Mentally, who would believe he was not? There was no man more charming to everyone else. Oh, to her, too! How could she therefore go to anyone and say what she knew, that in some hidden unsearchable fashion Gareth was a very sick man? What proof was there except that he had come back to her not the same Gareth who had gone away? She bent over him and kissed him sadly and then went back to her room and closed the door between them.

And in her own room Jennet flung herself upon her bed, tired at last.

"What a fool I am," she thought. "I know what I want." And thinking firmly of what she knew she wanted, she fell asleep.

"Your beau's waitin' for you, Miss Jennet."

In the laboratory Jennet looked down impatiently on the colored cleaning woman. She was late tonight, but she had determined to finish with the analysis of the tumor that she had seen Dr. Farland lift today out of a charity patient's body—not that its being a charity patient made any difference to him. He would have performed with the same meticulous care on any human body, rich or poor, young or old. He neither knew nor asked the details of that body's history beyond its disease.

"There are certain signs about this that lead one to decide against malignancy," he had said to the little circle of watching students. "But there is one strong argument for it. I shall expect reports from you by tomorrow afternoon."

He arranged the arteries and veins neatly, tied and clipped the ends and then stitched the cleanly cut flesh together again and superintended the expert bandaging which they all watched. He made a few tests.

"Patient is in first-rate condition," he remarked to them. "I doubt any aftereffects. You might drop in on her within the next twenty-four hours. Reports expected tomorrow morning." He nodded to the attending interns and walked toward the lavatory. "Good night," he said to his students.

The five young men and one girl filed out of the room. Jennet went straight to the laboratory. One young man followed her, she saw to her disgust. But the other four ran joyfully out into the sharp November evening. Tomorrow held plenty of time for them.

In the laboratory she reached the specimen first. It had been brought straight from the operating room. She ignored the young man, though she knew his name—

John Benton, a tallish, sandy-haired man from some western state. He waited for her but still she did not speak as she hurried to a microscope and desk in a far corner.

Then she had worked, feverishly, trying to isolate the malignant threadlike creatures that eluded her straight vision. She was sure it was there, having seen its shadow. At her feet she was aware at last of a crouched figure on hands and knees, swishing a wet rag, and then the voice.

"I'm not through yet, Lissy," she retorted.

"Yas'm," the voice said patiently. "Well, I'm just tellin' you. He's in his paw's office, waitin'. His paw's gone and thar he's sittin', watchin' thishyere do'."

Francis ought not, she thought angrily, to take this advantage of his father's office for their meeting. She had told him often and he always laughed.

"I believe in taking any advantage to see you," he had said. So he simply went on doing as he liked. Well, then, so would she.

She worked slowly for nearly an hour, firmly denying that impatient young man. At the opposite end of the laboratory John Benton worked as quietly concentrated. Once or twice when she lifted her hand to pick up a fresh slide she saw him, never looking at her. A cold, rather silent student in her classes, he was brilliant and without a tremor in mind or hand. He was ideal surgeon stuff. She envied him passionately for a moment. How glorious to be a man, unimpeded by anything! Then she put the thought aside proudly. She, too, could be unimpeded—if she so chose.

She worked another ten minutes. She was ready now, very nearly, to make up her mind on that thread-like evil. But could it, by a chance, be something else? She ought to make one more test.

"Hey you, Jennet Maclean!"

She turned, and there was Francis at the door behind her.

"Are they giving you overtime or what?"

"Sorry—I'm not through," she said shortly.

"Jennet, come on!" He sauntered over to her, his hands in his pockets. "I've been waiting ages."

She looked quickly at John Benton. He had not moved. "Francis, you know you haven't any business to come in here."

"But you don't come out!"

"I will when my work's done."

"When will that be?"

"I don't know—another half hour."

"I've waited over an hour."

"I didn't ask you to, Francis."

"You said—"

" 'You said!' You asked me to go out with you and I said *if* I got through. Well, I'm not through." She spoke almost angrily and turned to her microscope, aware of that still figure in the far corner.

Francis threw up his hands. "All right," he said, "I *am* through." He left her instantly and she heard the door slam behind her back. Quick-tempered and wilful, she thought. Well, let him be! The figure at the other desk had not moved.

She tried afresh to concentrate upon the slides and found she could not. The room was still and all her tools were perfect. But her mind would not do its work. It was running beyond the closed door, out of the building, following after those angry footsteps. Had she made Francis really angry at last?

"I do treat him abominably," she thought. "He hates waiting and he'd been waiting a long time and I did tell him I wanted to—if I could." She wanted to enormously, now that she thought of it. She wanted to run after him, to tell him she was sorry, to say she'd have dinner with him, dance, do anything he liked. The laboratory suddenly became intolerable to her, the slides unimportant. Besides, she actually had plenty of time tomorrow. Why had she come in here tonight to grind away like this when it was not necessary? She was doing well, keeping up with all the others. She had hurt Francis for nothing.

She began hastily to pack her slides and to cover the microscope and then to scrub up. A few minutes later she had her hand on the laboratory door. At that moment she looked across the room. For the first time John Benton had lifted his head. He was looking at her, a grim smile upon his desert-colored face. She stared back at him, unsmiling. What right had he to look at her like that? She all but flung the cry at him. Then she changed her mind. She would not speak to him. She banged the door and strode through the halls, ran down the steps and along the street.

She caught up with Francis two blocks from his father's house. Her step was a little longer than his, her pace a fraction more swift. Her eyes found him easily in the evening crowd, a slender figure in a tweed coat, his head hatless still, though the night was coming on cold.

"Francis," she said in an even clear voice. She touched his arm and he turned.

"Changed your mind?" he asked.

"I suppose so," she said unwillingly. But she was not sure how much.

They walked a block together. She waited for him to speak and when he did not she looked at him. He was still angry with her, very angry, she perceived. His delicate profile with its childlike, too sensitive lips was cold in the street light. She had slipped her arm in his, but he kept his hands in his pockets.

Her heart wavered between fear and its own anger. If he did not speak, then neither would she. She drew her hand from his arm and plunged it into her own pockets.

"Well, good night, Francis," she said abruptly. "I'll be going along home."

He stopped and so did she, an island of two, absorbed in their own hurt. People divided like water around a rock, stared at them and went on.

"That's what you want to do, is it?" he asked.

"Not particularly," she said, "but you don't seem to want to be with me."

His lips quivered. "You don't want to be with me."

"Yes, I do, Francis. But you don't seem to understand work."

"Yes, I do. I work every day myself. I stopped on my way back from the office."

"But my work—"

"Don't tell me your work's different," he broke in furiously. "That's what my father has told my mother since I was born."

"But it is in a way," she insisted. "When you're a doctor you can't think in terms of time. You can't leave at a regular time, it's not office work. It's—it's a life work."

"Sheer egotism," he said.

They looked at each other deeply.

"Well, if you think that," she said and drew in her breath. Her lips were quivering now and she could not control them. "I suppose we might just as well say goodbye," she said.

"I suppose so," he said.

They did not move.

"I've had too much of this doctor talk," he said. "It makes me tired. My father—"

"You forget my mother is a doctor," she said, "but it doesn't make me tired! It only makes me want to do my best. She—she's made me feel it's glorious work, worth every bit of my time and all my energy and everything I have!"

"What are you accusing me for?"

"Nothing!"

"You are—you're trying to make me feel less than you because I didn't want to be a doctor."

"Oh no, Francis!"

"That's the way you make me feel!"

"No—no—I'm only trying to make you understand why I feel I ought—"

"Well, I don't understand! I'll never understand—"

"I'm sorry," she said. Her low voice checked him. He stopped, wet his lips, fumbled in his pocket and found his cap and put it on his head. The wind was beginning to be cold.

"I was—was going to tell you something special tonight," he said. "That was why I waited for you."

Gazing at him steadily she did not answer.

"Now—I don't know," he said uncertainly.

She broke across this sharply. "Then I'm glad you're not telling me. I don't want you to say anything you're not sure you want to say."

"I do want to, but—"

"No!" she cried. "No—no!"

She turned and fled from him, homeward, as fast as she could. People stared at the tall girl whose face was set as though against weeping but she saw no one. She went swiftly down the avenue to her own house. Then she paused, and searched the way she had just come. If he had followed her—oh, if he had followed her! But he had not. The street was full of strangers. She opened the door and went in.

*   *   *

"I feel somehow that it's not really a merry Christmas for you, my darling," Dr. Maclean said conversationally, in the midst of Jennet's bubbling, restless talk. It was Christmas night, the end of a busy Christmas day —too busy, she thought. Jennet had crowded it full with a theater party besides. Now it was long after midnight.

She had listened, half smiling, as she had listened so many times to Jennet's talk at the end of a day, and then she had put the sharp diagnostic probe, penetrating at once to the center of a trouble she suspected rather than knew. So she had suspected all day, and for days, Jennet's unhappiness.

Jennet turned her back instantly on her mother and began brushing her hair. The dark curls flew out in an electric whorl around her head.

"I don't know what you mean," she said.

Her mother did not answer. She sat waiting and both of them knew that her mother understood this was pure self-defense. Jennet whirled around, half laughing, half crying.

"Yes, of course I do know what you mean! And of course you're right, Mother. Oh dear, why are you always so right?"

"Because I know you," her mother replied.

The tall girl stood uncertain for a few seconds. Then she flung the brush on the floor and dropped at her mother's feet.

"Might as well dig it out," she said. She hugged

her knees and faced the small figure in the big chair. So had many a soul faced that quiet gaze.

"Where has Francis been all day—and these last five weeks?" her mother asked.

"We had a quarrel."

"You didn't feel like telling me about it?"

"There was nothing to tell. I had to wait, for him to come back, for myself—to know if I want him back."

"Does he want to come back?"

"I don't know—if he doesn't, that simplifies things for me."

"Meaning you do want him back?"

Jennet shook her hair. "I don't know what I want! I always thought I did, but I don't."

"How is your work?"

"Swell—absolutely perfect! Exciting, every minute."

"But it's not quite enough?"

Jennet looked shrewdly at her mother. "Was it for you?"

Dr. Maclean hesitated. "No," she said gently.

"So, then," Jennet retorted.

"Is Francis—inevitable?" her mother probed delicately after a pause.

Jennet shrugged. "I seem to hanker after him," she admitted.

"Nobody in your class you like?"

Jennet considered. Some sort of a friendship was growing between her and John Benton, a queer grudging friendship because neither of them had any time for it, or wanted to have any time. But he had spoken to her the next day after her quarrel with Francis, and she, because she was still angry, had answered. It was before class. They were both a little early and so alone in the classroom.

"You report malignant?" he had inquired.

"No," she said. "I decided against it this morning. But I don't know what those stubby threads are."

"I don't, either. Not any malignancy I know, though."

They had fallen silent. Then he had spoken again, his amber eyes mischievous behind their sandy lashes.

"How's your persistent friend?"

"I don't know and care less," she had said loftily.

"Good," he had replied.

Since then they had spoken together a few times and once gone to a picture together. He told her in his gruff incomplete sentences that his father was a doctor in Arizona, and so was he going to be, but not a GP as the old man was. She asked him, trying not to be shy, what he thought of her being a surgeon.

"Why not?" he had replied. "If that's what you want," he had added.

"I like a fellow named Benton," she told her mother. "His technique is already wonderful."

"But?" her mother went on for her.

Jennet lifted her black lashes. "But he just isn't Francis." She laid her head on her knees a second and then lifted it restlessly. "What is it about one man in the world, not a man better than others and you know it, that simply sticks in your blood, so that as long as your heart beats he's there in you?''

Her mother did not answer.

''Were you so about Dad?'' Jennet asked.

''Yes,'' she replied.

''What did you do?''

''We married.''

''And you've been happy?''

Should she now tell Jennet? Was this the time, she asked herself, to tell Jennet everything?

''I can't imagine doing anything else than what I did,'' she said.

''You went on working.'' Jennet was pressing decision for herself out of the past.

''No, I gave it up. One doctor is as much as a marriage could stand, I thought then. Besides, I wanted above everything else to have my marriage a success.''

''Oh, of course,'' Jennet agreed warmly. ''Or it wouldn't be worth having.'' Her mind dealt with this a moment. ''And Dad—was he willing for you to give up your work?''

''He seemed to be.'' No, she would not tell Jennet of that deep sharp little hurt that she had instantly buried when Gareth had not protested the giving up of her work because she was the woman. ''Your father wanted our marriage to be a success, too,'' she said, ''and he honestly believed that it couldn't be if we both went on working.''

''But when did you change?''

Here was the question she had been dreading. She

took it bravely in both hands. "We didn't exactly change, dear. I had to work when he joined the army. He volunteered in the First World War, you know—I've told you that—not as a doctor but simply as a private in the French army. He couldn't stand what was going on over there. He wanted to protest with all his life. So I said, 'Go, if you feel it's right. I can work again.' So he went, and I began again, that's all. And somehow, well, I just didn't stop. He was only away a little over a year. He came back just before we declared war."

"Why?"

"He wasn't well—he'd had typhoid."

Told thus the facts hid the truth. She waited, but Jennet was satisfied. She asked no more. Whatever had happened before she was born was centuries gone.

"I don't know how Francis and I feel about each other." She lifted an eyebrow at her mother and tried to laugh. "Would you say a certain sort of anginal pectoral pain was true or false in my case?"

"If it persists, I'd call for fresh diagnosis," her mother answered.

They parted on that, or were ready to part had not the telephone on the little table by Jennet's bed rung loudly.

"Who, at this hour?" Jennet breathed. "It's probably for you. Some kid has had too much Christmas." She lifted the receiver and sank on the bed. "Francis!" she cried. "No—well, not quite! I was just going to- . . . No, I'm not sleepy, as far as that goes! . . . Where are you?"

Dr. Maclean, listening to the one-sided talk, observing every symptom of kindling eyes and flushed cheeks, began making her final private diagnosis.

"Of course I'll come—only *if* you were going to call, *why* not before? . . . Oh, well, maybe I wouldn't have, anyway, I'm coming—fifteen minutes!"

The receiver clanged, and Jennet leaped to her closet. "Moms, I'm going dancing! He wants me to— I'm not in the least tired—what'll I wear?"

"Your red taffeta," Dr. Maclean said. "It's still Christmas night." She sat there until she saw the tall dark girl flaming in the scarlet dress.

"Don't wait up for me," Jennet said, bending to kiss her mother.

"I shan't," her mother said tranquilly. She sat on a moment after Jennet had dashed from the room. Then she rose and began putting things away. She tidied the dressing table and straightened the bed, and laid out fresh pajamas. Jennet's red slippers she found in opposite corners of the room and she set them together by the chair. Then she went soberly to bed.

"All symptoms," she thought, "point to the inevitable."

But she lay awake a long time wishing with all her heart that Jennet had been a boy.

"He is inevitable," Jennet thought. She closed her eyes and swayed to the music. "I can't help this. I can't help anything that happens to me from now on. Everything in my life has to take this into account.''

"Sweet!'' Francis whispered, "have you missed me?''

"Yes,'' she said without opening her eyes.

"What would you have done if I hadn't called you tonight?''

"Gone on missing you.''

"I had to call you.''

"Then I'm glad you did.''

She was being perfectly reckless, she knew. Never, never had she yielded to him like this before. She had always refused to yield, laughing at him even while she listened. But the moment she saw him tonight she was so joyful, the whole wrong day was so instantly set right merely because they were together again, that she gave herself up to him. Whatever happened now, let it happen.

"Marry me, Jennet?''

She lost a step. Oh, this he had never asked before! Could it be asked like this, in the midst of dancing and music and a mad holiday crowd? She fended it off.

"Do you mean it, Francis?''

"I can't risk another month like this.''

She suddenly wanted to stop dancing and to get away from music. She wanted to be in cold quiet silence. "Let's get out of here.''

"All right.''

They found their coats and without speaking

waited for the elevator to take them to the ground.

"Up," the elevator man said.

Francis caught her hand. "Why not up?" he said. "There's the roof."

"Cold tonight, sir," the man said.

"We don't care," Francis said.

They stepped in and were lifted up, and stepped out on the empty terrace hung against the sky.

"Now a sheltered corner," Francis said.

She did not speak, letting herself be taken and led and guided. He found the shelter and then two chairs and dragged them there. "Now," he said, "we can talk."

But when they looked at each other there were no words. He leaned over to her and drew her into his arms.

"Ah, my beautiful," he whispered, and held her closer and closer, and she, yielding and nothing but yielding as she had never yielded herself since she was born, felt herself drawn utterly to him, until her lips were beneath his own. Out of the thick beat of her blood, out of the daze in her brain, she thought amazed, "This is what I want. Why didn't I know?"

She had to tell her mother. After Francis brought her home, she went straight upstairs to her mother's bedside. Then she hesitated a moment. Her mother's sleeping face looked pale and strangely aged in the dimness of the nightlight always burning in this room, lest there be a call.

"I oughtn't to wake her," she thought.

But her mother's eyes opened of their own accord. "Yes?" she said distinctly, instantly awake.

Jennet dropped to her knees. "Francis and I are going to be married," she whispered.

"Oh!" Her mother sat up. "But you didn't know, when you went—"

"I knew the moment I saw him."

"You feel sure?" They were whispering back and forth like conspirators.

"Sure as life."

"Well, then—" Dr. Maclean drew a deep breath. "That's your happiness."

"Yes."

She reached over and kissed the girl's dark fragrant hair. "God bless you, darling," she said aloud.

"He has," Jennet said simply. She gave her mother a strong handclasp and was gone.

She went to sleep almost instantly once she was in her bed. She was no longer tired, no longer restless. Life had fallen into place for her. She was going to be a man's wife, she and Francis would have children.

"I shall give up everything else," she thought. "I want to give up everything to him."

Rest was in the yielding, and peace, and the end of thought and strain. It was as if she had returned to some familiar place, whose ways were all known to her and old as the world. She was doing right and she slept, long and peacefully.

But it was not easy to tell Dr. Farland the next day.

"You must tell him at once," her mother said in the morning. "It's not fair to pretend you're going on for scholarship work when you're not."

This morning her mother seemed curiously remote. The warmth of their meeting in the night was gone. Perhaps it was only because she was hurried. She had been called on an out-of-town visit.

"See to your father, dear," she told Jennet. "He hasn't waked yet. I've left him a little note. I'll be back about midnight."

"Then he doesn't know?" Jennet asked.

"Know?" her mother repeated blankly. "Oh—about you—no, dear. You can tell him." And then she had said, as though it were much more important, "But you must tell Dr. Farland this very morning, if you've really decided to give up your work."

"I have," Jennet said definitely, and kissed her mother goodbye.

Why, she thought after her mother had gone, did it seem unimportant whether her father knew or not? She felt remorseful when he came into the dining room a few minutes after her mother had gone, and she hastened to pour his coffee.

"Hello, Dad darling," she said casually.

"Good morning, dear," he said. He looked so distant from all about him that she felt it difficult to begin, so she began quickly.

"Dad, I'm engaged to Francis."

He lifted his head.

"Francis?"

"You know, Francis Farland."

"Frank Farland's boy?"

"Yes, Dad."

She saw faint surprise on her father's face.

"Is he old enough to be married?"

"He's older by a year than I am, Dad." She laughed.

"I seem to remember him a boy," her father said. His head dropped again and he examined the egg on his plate. Then he picked up his fork.

"Don't you think it's nice, Dad?" She tried to make playfulness cover a gathering disappointment.

"I? Oh—very nice." He smiled at her unexpectedly. "But I won't think so if you are going away."

"We want our own home, Dad."

His smile faded.

"Yes, of course," he said and was silent.

She watched him for a few minutes. Was his gentleness, so pleasant to her in childhood, perhaps— emptiness? She put the question to herself and did not answer it. He was her father. She rose and kissed him.

"Do you have everything you want?"

"I? Yes, thank you."

"Then I'm off to see the bearded tiger in his den."

"You mean—"

"Dr. Farland," she said. "It's lucky I'm marrying his son, or he might not allow it."

She laughed and kissed him again and he gave her one of his slow smiles.

*   *   *

"Even you," Dr. Farland said.

"Even me," she replied. She had not dreamed that the telling could be so hard. Francis had not seen his father or mother. She found that out immediately.

"He's still abed," Dr. Farland had said. "On a holiday it's queer if I see him at noon."

"Well, then, it's up to me," she had said. So then she told him. "I'm going to give up my work because I'm going to marry Francis."

Dr. Farland's thick eyebrows drew down over his grey eyes.

"Even you?"

"Even me."

He cleared up his throat and pushed his chair back from the desk and took up a pencil.

"I'm hampered," he said. "It makes me furious to have a promising student give up in the middle of her first year. I'd not allow it if you weren't confusing the issue by marrying my own son. On the other hand, I can't tell you to keep on, for I wouldn't like it if my daughter-in-law kept on working. Besides, I confess it, I have a secret pleasure in knowing I'm still right— about women. I wish I'd never taken you in the first place. I knew I ought not."

"I mightn't be marrying Francis if I hadn't come in that day and you hadn't gone home and said I was— good-looking," she told him.

"I can't keep my mouth shut," he said ruefully. "Or else Francis is a fool about a good-looking girl."

They laughed. Then he sobered.

"Well, my dear, I suppose we'll have to cross you off for a dead loss as a surgeon, but I can't be sorry because I think you'll make a first-rate wife for my son."

"I want to," she said quickly.

"Then you will," he said.

She went away on that, aware of conflict in herself. She was glad it was over. Nothing could have been kinder than his handclasp, and yet she saw a distant irony in that grey gaze.

"I am right about women," he had said.

"Perhaps he is," she thought. But there was sting in the thought somewhere.

If there was, she had long forgotten it by her wedding day. Since she had nothing to wait for they were married soon, in April, after Lent was over. It was a pretty wedding, very quiet, in the living room of her own home. A few people she had always known were there, and their two families. Her father had never looked more calmly handsome, she thought, than when he stood to give her away. But her mother looked tired, too tired. She wished for a second that she and Francis had not planned quite so long a wedding trip. She had never been away from her mother a month in her life. But it was too late to change anything. Her marriage to Francis had decided everything. Besides Francis was first now and always.

For some impetuous reason she had sent John Benton a wedding invitation. She thought of it as she turned to face the little crowd. He was not there, her eye saw in an instant. Well, it did not matter now.

"Dearly beloved," old Dr. Hopewell chanted in his rich voice, "we are together today, in the sight of God and man—" She drew close to Francis at the words. Never to part again, she thought, and stood, her shoulder touching his.

II

"PERFECTLY WELL and perfectly happy," she said distinctly, looking up at her mother.

She had been married a year, and she had had her first baby an hour ago. A little girl, they said. In a moment they would bring her in again for her to hold. She had had a glimpse of a small dark-haired thing in a blanket, but she had been too dazed with drugs to give more than a sleepy murmur. Now she felt perfectly well.

"Good," her mother said. She smiled. "Your technique, I might say, was perfect."

"I'd have been ashamed if it hadn't been," Jennet said. She waited a moment. Then she asked what she had been wanting to ask from the first. "Where is Francis?"

The nurse answered quickly, "He'll be here at any moment, he just telephoned."

Jennet did not look at her mother. "Tell them I want to wait until he comes before they bring me the baby. I want us to see her together." She turned quick defensive eyes to her mother. "I told Francis not to come until it was all over."

"Very wise," her mother murmured.

"He hates messy things," Jennet said, "so why drag him into it?"

"Why indeed?" her mother echoed. She examined Jennet's chart. Everything was perfect. "I think I'll run along now and let you rest," she said, "until Francis comes." She bent to kiss Jennet's cheek. "I'll be back before night."

"Thank you, Mother," Jennet said.

When her mother was gone she felt suddenly listless and weak. Of course Francis ought to have been here. There was no use trying to hide anything from her mother. Still, there was nothing to hide except the fact that Francis was unpredictable. She had learned throughout this year that she simply had to accept it, that she could never be quite sure of what he would do or neglect to do.

"I'll sleep a little while," she told the nurse. "But wake me when my husband comes."

"I will," the nurse said.

When she woke she knew she had slept a long time. She opened her eyes and saw the nurse sitting there in the darkened room.

"Has my husband not come?" she asked.

"No, not yet," the nurse replied gently.

Jennet did not speak again. There was no use in pretending now that she was not simply furious with Francis. How could he, today of all days—then she schooled herself. She would wait, she would be patient, she would let him explain before she judged him. There had been grief enough between them because time after time he had not measured up to her expectation of him. If only her mother did not come back before Francis came! She lay for a half hour, tense and unable to rest. The nurse got up and took her temperature.

"Would you like anything special for your dinner, Mrs. Farland?"

"Is it dinner time?"

"Seven thirty is the time for private patients. It's about seven."

"I don't care what I have, thanks."

The nurse tiptoed out, and Jennet, left alone, felt like crying and did not. She simply was not going to cry any more because Francis disappointed her. There had been enough of that, too—not that she had let him see. She had been bitterly ashamed of herself in this year that she could cry so easily. But then perhaps it had been partly because of the baby's beginning so soon. Still, she had eagerly wanted the baby.

At the end of the hall the nurse was telephoning softly.

"Dr. Farland? This is Mrs. Farland's nurse. I think she's fretting, sir, because her husband hasn't been in."

"You mean he hasn't been there at all?"

"No, sir."

"Goddam—" the telephone clattered at her ears.

Twenty minutes later the door of Jennet's room burst open.

"Sweetheart, I could kick myself!"

He was there—he had her in his arms.

"Oh, Francis—careful, darling! I've only just—"

"Of course I telephoned. I knew everything was all right. I was held up."

"Sure you don't mind she's a girl?"

"All I care about is that you are all right. Sure you are, darling? Was it worse than you thought?"

"Pretty bad, but of course Mother's wonderful." Strange, now that he was here, that the day she had spent in giving birth seemed a thing between her mother and herself, and not Francis!

"I've not let them bring the baby until you came, darling." She pressed the bell frantically. Now she could not wait for her baby. But her nurse had already seen Francis coming in. She opened the door, smiling, the small bundle in her arms, and laid it beside Jennet and went away again.

They were suddenly shy, she and Francis, before this small solemn creature they had made. She drew aside the white blanket, and they gazed down on the little sleeping face. Neither of them spoke for a few seconds.

"I say," Francis spoke first, his voice slightly shocked. "We'll never be alone together any more!"

"No," she laughed at him.

"Will you like that?" he inquired.

"It's a little late if I don't," she retorted. Then she felt bubbling over with joy and laughter and love. "Oh, Francis," she cried, "what would I do if you were like anybody else?"

Dr. Farland, dining late and alone with his wife, was exploding over the roast beef.

"I tell you, Edith, I sometimes wonder whether the boy's any good. My God, when that nurse called me up and told me he hadn't even been there!"

"Wait, please, Frank!" Mrs. Farland's prettily arched eyebrows lifted with meaning toward the maid.

Dr. Farland exploded again. "Good God, Della knows Francis as well as we do!"

Della retired with wise swiftness and closed the door softly into the kitchen.

"I don't think it's right to talk before servants," Mrs. Farland murmured.

"Della stopped being a servant twenty years ago," Dr. Farland retorted. "What I was trying to say, Edith, was that Francis didn't go near his wife until I told him to get the hell up there to the hospital, that he'd been a father for five hours and had shown not the slightest sign of behaving like one. What's the matter with you?" He stopped, struck by the peculiar immobility of Mrs. Farland's extremely pretty face.

"I don't mean to defend Francis, but I do think you

ought to find out what he was doing. Perhaps they wouldn't let him leave his office. Maybe he had a client there or something.''

Dr. Farland grunted. ''The biggest deal in the world couldn't have kept me away from you when he was born.''

''But you're a doctor yourself,'' she said. ''You knew what I'd been through. Besides,'' she smiled at him with sweetness, ''you knew I couldn't do without you. I'm not like Jennet. I suppose Francis thought that Jennet was something like a doctor herself. I shouldn't be surprised Jennet told him to stay away. And her mother was there.''

Dr. Farland listened doubtfully. ''Well, maybe,'' he granted her. ''Still—by the way, have you sent any message, Edith?''

''Certainly,'' she said quickly. ''I sent a dozen red roses for Jennet and a bunch of tiny pink roses for the baby the moment I heard. I had left word at the hospital I was to be called at once.''

''Well—'' Dr. Farland broke off and fell to eating. How many times had he been thus gently and yet finally silenced by arguments about Francis, reasonable and yet somehow not quite valid? What was this speciousness that was in the best of women? He had never had time—never taken time, perhaps, to find out. And now he never would. Years ago he had learned to take Edith as she was, still the prettiest and sweetest girl he had ever known. When she told him that night that Francis was born that she never wanted another child, he could scarcely blame her. Her little frame had been almost too fragile for its single task. He had simply seen to it that she had her way. It was the only way to handle women —give them their way and take your own.

Jennet, at the door of their apartment, turned to the nurse carrying the baby.

"Let me take her in for the first time," she said. She took the little bundle carefully in her arms.

"Sure you are strong enough?" the nurse asked.

"I'd never know I'd had a baby if I didn't have it!"

She stepped over the threshold proudly. It was the middle of the morning and Francis couldn't be here, but she had thought that over and decided that she'd rather be home with the baby all settled when he came back. And this nurse—she wasn't going to need this nurse, in spite of her mother's insisting on paying for her for two weeks. She didn't want her mother to pay for things. It was her pride to be able to live on what Francis was able to provide for her.

At this moment she caught sight of her mother's little figure in the kitchen.

"Mother!" she shouted. "What are you doing here?"

Dr. Maclean came briskly out of the tiny kitchen with a cup in her hand. "I came in to stir you up something," she said. "I wanted to see for myself how you are. Drink this, please." She set the cup down and took the baby expertly from Jennet's arms. This little creature she had come to know very well. Without a word to anyone she had stolen into the baby's ward day after day to sit holding her in her arms, examining the small features. How she had wanted more children! Now Jennet would give them to her. The baby yawned with enjoyment and looked up into her face, and she laughed.

"They love to yawn," she said.

"Do they? How do you know, Mother?"

"Oh, I'm sure they do."

Jennet laughed and took up the cup. "This is good. What is it?"

"Malted chocolate. You must drink it twice a day for a while."

"That won't be hard. Mother, I shan't want this nurse!"

"Two weeks."

"No! I want the house to myself." House, she always called this five-room apartment, because some-day she and Francis would have a house with a yard.

"I wish you wouldn't be so purse-proud," her mother remarked. "You're going to rob me of much pleasure if I can't do little things for this dear child."

"I don't want Francis to think I'm not satisfied with what he can do."

"That's nonsense. He knows you are perfectly capable of earning money if you're not satisfied. If you don't, isn't it proof?"

Jennet shook her head.

"I want him to know we *need* things."

Her mother looked at her shrewdly. "My dear, you're not trying to make him over into what he isn't?"

"Of course not! But he has so much ability, Mother. He could do anything he liked. He's brilliant, really. But he doesn't care. He works just enough to get his salary. He doesn't seem to care whether he is getting on or not."

"Some people don't," her mother said. "I don't believe you can change them."

"I can't understand it, then," Jennet said almost harshly. She took off her hat and smoothed back her hair with quick strong hands—surgeon's hands, her mother thought as she always did when she saw them. "If he won't go ahead for himself," Jennet went on, "then he must for us. This isn't to be our only child. I want six. I'm going to have them in pairs—another next year, and then two years between the next pair."

"You're very sure of yourself, darling," her mother said. "Does Francis—"

Jennet broke in. "Francis always wants me to have what I want. It's simply that he lacks ambition for himself. He can't seem to get up in the morning in time to get to work, and when he's in the office he doesn't get through in time to get home early. I know exactly what happens. He talks and enjoys anybody who comes in— chats with the stenographers probably when there's no one else. Everybody adores him and wastes his time but nobody really appreciates him as I do or believes in him as I do. I know what he could be if he would."

"You love him," her mother said quietly.

"Terribly," Jennet whispered. Her eyes filled with tears, to her own astonishment.

"I know," her mother said.

The baby began suddenly to fret and the nurse appeared at the door.

"If you please, Mrs. Farland, it's time to nurse the baby."

Jennet leaped to her feet. "Oh, I forgot!" she cried.

"I'll take the baby," the nurse said. She led the little procession into the bedroom and Dr. Maclean stood in the doorway watching Jennet.

"She's forgotten everything," she thought gratefully. But it was like Jennet to devote herself entirely to one thing, even to nursing her child. "I must go now, dear," she said aloud.

Jennet looked at her vaguely, the baby at her breast. This rite, so new, was filled with wonder still. She could think of nothing else for the moment.

"Oh," she said, "then, thank you, Mother—for everything, and goodbye!"

"Goodbye, dear," her mother said. She took an instant longer to impress upon her memory this new picture of Jennet, to add it to all the long procession of pictures since she had held Jennet, herself a baby, at her own breast. But she had never been so beautiful as Jennet now was, bending tall and passionate above her little child.

"I'm glad she can have all the children she wants," Dr. Maclean thought, and trudged away to work.

"Happy?" Jennet asked him.

The house was clean, the nurse gone at last, the baby asleep. She and Francis were alone and the dinner over. She never washed the dishes at night. In the morning it could be done quickly, when Francis was gone. They had their dinner in dignity and grace and went into the living room. Later when Francis was reading the evening paper she would slip out and stack the dishes. Everything was organized, she liked to think, for his comfort.

Francis sat in his favorite chair and pulled her to his knees.

"Of course—say, sweet, when are we going to be free again in the evenings?"

"Any time," she said quickly. "The only difference is that I have to know in the morning to get my girl."

She had arranged for freedom, too. There was an agency in the city that provided for just such things as free evenings for young parents—expensive, but she'd squeeze it in somehow.

"By the way," she said casually, "any chance of the big boss stepping you up a little?"

"Gosh, I wish he would," Francis said. His

charming lazy smile crept to his lips as he lit a cigarette. He shifted her a little on his knee.

"Heavy?" Jennet inquired—only she wasn't any heavier! She was taking care about that.

"No—well, you're nobody's chicken."

She slipped off at that and sat on the rug and leaned her head against his knees. "Is there anything you could do to get promoted?"

"I don't know that there is." He took two deep draughts of smoke.

"Isn't anybody getting ahead?"

"There have been one or two fellows, but I'm not going to kill myself the way they do. Life isn't worth it."

"We could do with a bit more, at that."

"I thought your mother—"

"I can't take things from Mother, Francis. She's worked for every penny she has. Why should we let her?"

"I could talk to Dad."

"No! Besides, for what? We can't depend on other people to pay our daily bills. If it were an emergency—"

He laughed. "I call a baby an emergency of the first order."

"No, it isn't," she retorted. "It's a natural procedure." She got up and sat on a chair and lit a cigarette for herself. What would he say if she said, "Perhaps I had better go to work, too?" Agree with her, probably!

She controlled her irritation and waited for it to pass. Then she spoke. "Darling, would you care to talk over with me the possible ways you could rise in your job? I might be able to help, somehow." She made an effort to smile. "I used to be quite good in school. I even got a summa cum laude at college."

But he shook his head. "I don't want to talk office when I come home at night." He looked at her, coaxing her. "Oh, darling, don't be dissatisfied with me!" His were such clear and tender eyes that love swept her clean.

"I'm not," she said. "How can I be, when I love you so?"

But even in his arms her mind began almost at once to justify her ambition for him. She loved him so much that she wanted to be proud of him, too. She needed to be proud of him, because she wanted to love him more and more. And she could love him more, yes, more than she did now, if he would let her.

"That's my girl," he said heartily. He smiled at her and reached for the evening paper folded on the table.

III

FRANCIS WAS THERE promptly enough, Dr. Maclean thought to herself, when Jennet's second baby was born a year after Patsy. She came out of Jennet's room and there he was, looking very debonair in his linen suit. He had yellow roses in his hand.

"Is she all right?"

"Perfectly," Dr. Maclean said. "It's another little girl."

"That's nice, for Patsy," he said. "I rather hoped for a girl."

She liked him for honestly meaning this. Some men would have wanted a son.

"You can go in after a few minutes," she said, "Jennet is not quite out of ether, yet. I'll be back later."

"Fine," he said, and sat down.

Different, she thought, from a year ago, and wondered why. She went on down the hall. Then she stopped and turned back to him. "Patsy, by the way, is behaving beautifully at my house."

"Good," he said heartily. "Jennet will be glad to hear that. But she's a nice little thing."

"Adorable," she agreed, and started on again. She found herself eager to get home these nights, now that there was the little dark-eyed girl there. She took a taxicab from the hospital and entered her door eagerly.

"Everything all right?" she asked Mary. Mary was doing very well for a maid not used to children. Patsy liked her.

"The little girl's fine, Madame," Mary said.

"I'll come in as soon as I've washed," Dr. Maclean said. She washed, and then saw Gareth in his room getting ready for bed.

"Jennet's very well," she said.

"I'm glad to hear it," he said.

"The new baby is a beautiful little thing—very blonde, this time, like Francis."

"Did Francis mind not having a boy?" he asked.

She glanced at him quickly. "Did you think he would?"

"I don't know," he hesitated, fumbling at the buttons on his pajamas. She went over to him and buttoned them quickly. "Those skilful hands of yours," she said smiling, "and so stupid with buttons!" She wished instantly that she had not spoken. His eyes grew blank and she could feel him shrink from her. "Dear Heart, don't be hurt," she said. "I didn't mean anything."

"I feel—very useless," he whispered.

"You're all I have," she said gently. She put him to bed then like a child, like a sick old man, and tucked him in. "Shall I put the light out or will you read?"

"I don't feel like reading. Angie, will you bring me a drink of water?"

"Yes, dear." She fetched it and stood while he drank. He handed her back the glass.

"I don't like you to wait on me." He smiled at her faintly.

"Nonsense," she said. "You wait on me. You're always finding my glasses for me."

"That's different," he said. "I ought to do that. Good night, Angie, dear wife."

"Good night, dear husband." They kissed and she put out the light and went toward the nursery, puzzled again in the deep mystery of her life. He was so punctilious in his behavior toward her, so careful to ask nothing of her in small ways of service. She had cried one day, she who never cried, when she had come upon him sewing on a button. He had, she found, bought himself a little sewing kit somewhere.

"Gareth, why didn't you ask me to sew on your button?"

"I don't like to bother you," he had murmured.

Never had she been so wounded. "But you can't bother me. I love to do things for you. Here, let me!" She had taken the needle and garment from his hands and sewed the button on quickly and firmly. Then she had picked up the sewing kit. "I'm going to take this away from you," she had said, trying to be playful. "Anyone would think you hadn't a wife."

And yet year after year he had let her go on earning their living, paying for the house, for Jennet's education, for all the life they had begun, together. She had learned now never to ask him a question about his work, when he was going to begin, whether he was going to begin. She could not bear again that agony in his eyes, that low, distressful voice, "I—don't know."

She had learned at last that he spoke the truth—he did not know. So long ago he had come home from France, hiding in his breast some secret which he had not told her. Then she did not even suspect it by imagination. She had been only absorbed in her joy that he had come home. As soon as he was well, she had told herself, everything would be as it had always been. She waited for his real return, and went on working. As soon as he was well, she would give up her office and stay at home and have another baby and then another and another—four children, maybe six. People like Gareth and her ought to have children.

She waited until his body was well again and outwardly he was the strong-looking, serious young man who had left her so suddenly one day to go to France. Then she waited longer until he would tell her that he was ready to work again. Then when waiting went on she had put questions to him in small gentle ways. Should she renew the lease on her office for another year, or would he— Did he want her to stay at home more, or had she better go on? She had put out her questions like pleading hands. But there was no answering hand—only hesitation, and then after the long pause, his low cry, "I don't—know." What had happened in him? She struggled to discover and could not because he shrank away from her into that dim self of his behind the walls of fog between them. She gave up at last, and putting away forever her woman's life, she had gone to work in earnest. And now she had learned. She had learned merely to be thankful that she could take his place. She put it all aside from her now as she had so many times, and opened the door of the room that had once been Jennet's. Once more a little dark-haired girl slept here. Mary was there, tucking the baby in. Dr. Maclean went over to the bed. Patsy lay, bathed and rosy and full of sleep.

"Bun," she said, and held up a large white velvet rabbit.

"She wouldn't take her nap, Madame," Mary said soberly, "and so I had to go over and fetch her Bun. She kept sayin' 'Bun—Bun,' and I took the latchkey Mrs. Farland left here, ma'am, and left the new girl in charge while I went myself. I remembered that she had the rabbit once when she came with her mother."

"That was good of you, Mary," she said.

Mary did not answer. She seemed subdued, Dr. Maclean thought, aware always of any human being near her.

"Are you getting a cold, Mary?" she asked.

"No, Madame."

"Your eyes are red." Dr. Maclean examined the familiar faithful face. "If you are, you oughtn't to be taking care of Patsy."

"Oh, Madame!" Mary cried. She put her apron to her eyes.

"Why, Mary," Dr. Maclean said. She drew her out of the child's sight. "I've never seen you like this!"

"I've never been like this," Mary sobbed. "How to tell you, I don't know, poor Miss Jennet—poor innocent child, havin' her second—not knowin'—"

"Mary, control yourself." Dr. Maclean spoke sharply. When these composed English serving women broke down they were worse than any others. "Come into my office in ten minutes," she ordered. "We must not terrify Patsy."

"No, Madame," Mary whispered and crept from the room.

She kissed the little girl good night and sang her a

song which Jennet had liked. Then she opened the window and went to her office and waited.

Try as she did, she could not quite control her own terror. Mary had seen something in Jennet's house that should not have been there. While Jennet was away, sure not to come back, something was there.

The door opened and Mary stood before her. Dr. Maclean leaned forward on her desk. "Now, if you will tell me, Mary, exactly what you saw."

Mary lifted a corner of her apron.

"Don't cry, please," Dr. Maclean said clearly, and she dropped it again.

"Madame, the maid Miss Jennet—Mrs. Farland took to look after things while she was away, she says Mr. Farland isn't there at all—sleeps out, she says."

"Sleeps out!" Dr. Maclean said. "I think you must be mistaken, Mary."

"No, that I'm not, ma'am," the woman said. She hesitated, then burst out, "Oh ma'am, ought I to tell you or not? It's Miss Jennet I'm thinking of."

"Of course you must tell me," Dr. Maclean said.

"She—the maid, I mean—she says he's—Mr. Farland's took up with another woman."

"Mary!" Her voice, forbidding, frightened, brought the blood to the woman's sallow cheeks.

"She showed me two letters, ma'am, she'd found 'em in the pockets of his suit. I saw 'em. The name was Christine." She coughed behind her hand. "I wouldn't demean myself to repeat what they said, ma'am. But they'd—been together—so to speak, if you know what I mean.''

She raised her eyes and saw Dr. Maclean's face. ''Oh ma'am!'' she cried. Her eyes filled with tears. She burst into wailing sobs and throwing her apron over her head she rushed from the room.

Behind her Jennet's mother sat motionless, leaning on her desk. It was impossible not to believe what Mary had said—yet impossible to imagine it. And yet Jennet was not to be told, must not be told, unless it was true. Her whole being recoiled from asking Francis. No, she could not face without rage that pleasant voice, that charming, coaxing, laughing manner. To whom could she turn? Where was the judge of what was the truth? And even if it were true, must Jennet be told? Could Francis be frightened into goodness again? Did he love Jennet still?

She sat there without sense of time, searching for wisdom. She had no one. All her life long she had depended on herself. She could have done for herself still if it had not been Jennet's life, lying in the palm of her hand.

''But Francis has parents, too,'' she thought. They would suffer over this. How much harder for them than for her, whose child had committed no fault! She felt tears rise suddenly to her tired eyes at the thought of Jennet's goodness.

''She's so good,'' she whispered, the tears running down her face. ''She gave up her work for him, even, because she didn't want anything to interfere between them.'' She pulled herself sharply together. Of course, Dr. Farland must know. She would tell him in the morning. She rose and was too exhausted to go to bed. She stretched herself on the couch and pulled her old green steamer rug over her and fell asleep.

The two doctors sat face to face, each hiding from the other. Dr. Farland's face was grey.

"If this is true, Dr. Maclean, my son is a skunk."

"Don't judge until you know," she replied.

"Women do write the damndest letters to handsome men—but I shan't defend him because he is my son—I want you to know that."

"I am sure of it." She rose, put out a small, cold hand. He took it and clung to it out of sheer distress.

"Is Jennet all right this morning?"

"I have only telephoned. They said she was wonderfully well."

"Was *he* there yesterday?"

"Yes—with roses." She pulled her hand away and smiled at him sadly and went away.

Dr. Farland touched a bell. "Cancel all my appointments," he told the nurse when she appeared.

"But, doctor—"

"Parcel them out to the other two doctors," he said. "Tell them I'm sick—got to have a few hours off."

He jammed on his hat, strode past the half dozen people already in his waiting room and hurried down to the street. Then he looked at his watch. Half past eleven. He'd better take a cab straight to the boy's office and walk in. He hooked his thumb at a cab, jumped in, shouted the street address and sat slumped on his spine, his hat over his eyes. He'd go straight in and fire the thing at the boy like a pistol. "You skunk, you—your wife in the hospital with your child—" Over and over he said it, "You skunk, you—"

The cab jerked to the sidewalk and he threw the man a coin and stalked into the building.

"Seventh," he said.

"Are you expected?" the clerk asked blandly, on the seventh floor.

Dr. Farland pushed back his hat and glared at him. "I'm his father, goddamn you!"

"I'm sorry, sir," the clerk said hastily. "He—Mr. Farland hasn't come in yet this morning. He said he could be reached at home if anything important—"

"Never mind!" Dr. Farland whirled and stormed back to the elevator. Still home. At noon. He didn't want to know why, didn't want to think of it. The skunk. The low rotten stinking—

He was in the apartment house at last, brushing aside the guard in the lobby, ringing furiously for the elevator, shouting the floor at the elevator man, banging on the door. He waited the fraction of a moment and kicked it. Then he saw Francis, robe flung over his pajamas, his fair hair tumbled and his eyes full of sleep.

"Why, Dad," he said uncertainly.

"You damned low rotten stinking skunk!"

Francis stood perfectly still, staring at his father. So, somehow the old man knew!

"Sit down," he said cooly.

"I won't sit down!" his father roared. "I won't dirty myself by staying here! What have you been up to while your wife's away? What sort of a—oh God!"

He took out his handkerchief and wiped his face. Then he looked at his son and felt weak.

"Boy, is it true?" he whispered.

Francis did not speak or move.

"Can't you say something—anything?" his father begged.

"No," Francis said.

"Not even if it's true?"

"It's my own business," Francis said sullenly.

"Then it is true," his father whispered. "God, I didn't believe it. I was mad but I didn't really believe it. That common piece—after Jennet! But it's true." He felt sick and not able even to be angry any more. "Got to go home," he muttered.

He turned blindly and rang for the elevator, and knew that Francis stood there watching him. But he did not move. He had to get home where he could lie down. The elevator came and he went in and leaned against the corner and shut his eyes. The thing nearly made him drop but he stepped out somehow.

"Ole man's had a big night," he heard the elevator man snigger behind his back. But he paid no heed. Into a cab, his eyes shut—home, his latchkey in the door—he staggered into the hall and saw his wife dimly in the room beyond.

"Edith," he said distinctly, "Francis is a skunk." Then he crumpled to the floor and was instantly unconscious.

The telephone was ringing without stop. Francis unloosed Christine's arms from about his neck.

"Got to see what that is, sweet," he said gently.

"Oh golly, let it ring," she whispered. She clung to him and he waited a moment. It kept ringing.

"I'll have to go," he said.

He left her curled up on the couch, a little thing, he thought tenderly, who had never had much in life. He had given her all the happiness she had ever had, she had told him many times. She lay looking up at him, blonde and blue-eyed.

"You're wonderful!" she whispered, and he smiled.

But the telephone kept ringing. He went to it and snatched off the receiver and shouted into it, "Hello! Hello!"

"Francis, darling!" He heard his mother's weeping voice. "Come home quickly, dear. Your father's had a stroke!"

"Gosh, Mother," he groaned, "I'll be there as fast as I can." He put up the receiver. "I've got to go," he said to Christine.

"Aw—" she began.

"It's my father," he said. "He's very sick." He hurried into his coat and hat. Upon the couch Christine did not stir. He looked at her uneasily.

"Better be getting down to the office, sweet."

"What's the use if you're not there?"

"We're not quite ready to tell the world yet," he said.

She sprang up suddenly and into his arms. "Promise you'll never leave me? Promise you won't change your mind?"

"Promise," he whispered. Oh, she was a soft little thing, small as a child! Her head was under his arm.

"I haven't anybody—only you! I never loved anybody before you. I'll never love anybody else."

"I know."

"Oh Frank, you're so strong—hold me!"

He held her hand. A man could make a mistake—plenty of men made mistakes. A man had a right to his own life, and here was a woman who needed him, who believed in him, just as he was, without continually wanting him to be something else.

"You're my boss and always will be," she said, smiling up at him. "When you're my husband you'll still be my boss."

"Sweet!" he muttered. "I'll be at the office as soon as I can get there." He pulled her arms away and hurried out of the door. His heart was molten in his breast. Nothing—nobody would make him give up Christine.

"Hurry," he said to the cab driver.

"That's what they all say," the cab driver replied.

"I don't think I'd better go in to see him," he said to his mother. Then he decided that he would tell her the truth. "Father is angry at me, Mother, and perhaps you'd better know. The fact is"—he searched from one pocket to another for his cigarettes—"I've found I can't be happy with Jennet. Dad knows. He was upset about it this morning."

"Francis!" His mother sat down quickly. "Dear, what are you saying?"

"I'm sorry, Mother. I know it's a shock. It's been to me, too."

"But Francis, you haven't—it's terribly sudden!"

"Not for me, I'm afraid. I've known for months."

"But Jennet's just had your second baby!"

"Mother, don't be so old-fashioned. Of course I've—fought against my feelings, tried to be just the same to Jennet."

She was beginning to cry and he was glad of it. It always meant she was softening and that she would try to understand him.

"Oh dear, oh dear—that's why he called you what he did!"

He did not ask what it was his father had called him. Instead he went to his mother and put his arm about her shoulders.

"Mother, you'll like Christine."

She looked up out of her handkerchief. "Who's Christine?"

"Christine Bland. I'm going to marry her."

"Francis! You didn't say there was somebody else!"

"That's how I know, Mother."

She sobbed again. He said gently, "Mother, you must help me. The rest of them will all be against Christine. But you've always understood. It's nothing against Jennet, Mother. She's fine, she's always been. But Christine's like you—gentle and understanding. She loves me, too—the way you do, I think. Jennet is never satisfied with me. She doesn't really like the sort of man I am. She's always wanting me to be something else. Now Christine—well, she thinks I'm wonderful."

His mother was wiping her eyes. He felt her hand move toward his and cling to it.

"You and Christine would have a great deal in common," he said, "and you and Jennet never have."

"Your mother bores me," Jennet had told him frankly. "She's sweet, but I'm used to women like my mother."

"Jennet always tries to be nice to me," his mother faltered.

"Christine wouldn't have to try," he said warmly.

"Well," his mother said uncertainly, "I don't know."

"Stick by me, Mother," he urged. "You always have!"

"Well, I'll see," she said sadly. "But we'll have to wait until your father is well."

At the door the doctor appeared. "You may come in," he said. "Dr. Farland is returning to consciousness."

If Dr. Farland had been well, would he have been so weak? Jennet's mother, sitting in his bedroom a few days later, knew the question could never be answered. What she had to take into account was what he was now, wonderfully recovered, but somehow not the same. A slight shock—but was any shock ever slight?

"I shall have to tell Jennet today," she said. "She is to come home tomorrow. I am taking her to my house, and she does not know it."

Jennet's mother was looking old, Dr. Farland thought, very old. He'd be all right again in a couple of days. There was scarcely any thickness left in his tongue when he spoke. But he was tired—tired. Everything made him tired.

"I've done all I could, but the boy's mind is made up," he said. "It's nothing sudden."

"I don't believe Jennet has an inkling of it," she said. "She's devoted to him."

"Too devoted, maybe," Dr. Farland grunted. "She's got a lot of energy."

She pondered this. There was, perhaps, something in it. Then her mind rejected utterly any fault in Jennet.

"I know she has tried very hard to be a good

wife," she said distinctly. The words were old-fashioned, but let them be so, she thought. In the old-fashioned sense Jennet had tried to be a good wife. Her home was beautifully kept, her husband always consciously put first. "Francis will like that—Francis won't like that—" how often she had heard Jennet deciding everything in her life in that way.

"Well, yes," Dr. Farland said. He thought of the hours that Edith had talked to him. She had persuaded him that he must see Francis. "No one must break up *our* little family," she had said, and so he had let Francis come in and after a while he had felt something Edith said. They were one family, he and Edith and Francis, and at last he had listened to the boy's side. There was a side, but how could you tell Jennet's mother? His doctor was at the door at this moment and there could be no more talk and he was glad of it.

"I wish you'd tell Jennet," he said, "and tell her we're terribly sorry—Edith and I. But it's inevitable, I'm afraid, and nobody's fault. Tell her we're fond of her and always will be."

His doctor came in and Jennet's mother rose.

"I will," she said.

"Well, well!" the doctor cried at the sight of his patient. "Not rushing things, are we? How do you do, Dr. Maclean? Nice day, isn't it? Did you ever see anything as tough as Frank Farland?" He and Frank were old friends, and Edith had told him the sad state of affairs—had to, to explain the shock. He had never cared about women being doctors, but now he wanted to be nice to this woman.

The saddest of smiles touched her lips. "He's made a remarkable recovery," she said. She smiled again, and slipped out of the room.

In the hall she hesitated, not, she told herself later, to listen. She paused, her footfall silent upon the thick carpet, only to think what next she might do for her child. She had seen neither Francis nor his mother. It had not seemed possible. Now, she asked herself, ought she not to see them and discover, if she could, why Francis was determined—if he was? And then at this moment she heard Dr. Farland's heavy voice, answering words she had not heard.

"After all, men don't like to be managed and one must remember," Dr. Farland was saying, "Jennet comes from a home where the woman is the boss."

There was the sound of answering laughter. She heard it as she heard the words, like a blow from a trusted hand. Dr. Farland, Gareth's friend, her friend, she had always thought, had he so little understood all those long years? Did he only see Gareth as the common henpecked man—and her as the sort of woman who would do so common a thing? She had been too successful, she thought drearily, in hiding Gareth's failure from everybody. She had tried to shield him and now she was blamed for him.

Suddenly she was filled with fury. No, this was too much to bear. She would go in and tell the truth. "I heard what you said—it's not true. I never tried to boss

Gareth—never, never! I've loved him and adored him. I wanted him to let me stay at home and have children and—and be his wife . . .'' She turned quickly, determined to go into that room and tell the truth to the two men, how all these years she had hidden Gareth's change, and that she might keep it hidden had worked and earned and kept the house paid for and Jennet taken care of and educated—what would have happened to them all if she had not been able to do this? Their laughter echoed in her ears.

She stopped, too wounded for self-defense. If a friend knew her no better than this nothing she could now say would do her any good. No, to speak would be to uncover all that she had tried to keep hidden for Gareth's sake. She hesitated one instant, then she turned and stole downstairs and out of the door. There was no use in seeing Francis or his mother. What mercy could she hope for, when just now she had been given none? She would go to the hospital and tell Jennet as quickly and simply as she could.

Hospital rooms, she thought, ought to be more cheerful so that when there was bad news the eyes could turn to pictures upon blank walls.

"I can't believe it," Jennet gasped.

"No, darling. I couldn't, at first."

If there were a picture on that blank wall of a quiet meadow, a brook, a tree, anything to give her eyes somewhere to look except at this suffering face!

"But Mother, we've always been perfectly happy!"

"He says he hasn't been for months, Jennet. His father told me so. She's been his secretary for a year."

Better the blank wall than Jennet's face! She knew from long bearing of pain that she must not take Jennet in her arms. She hated so to cry—she always had, this proud child of hers.

"That silly woman! Why, Mother, she's older than Francis. She's thirty if she's a day! And not even pretty!"

She did not answer this. If Francis were that sort of a man, what did these comparisons matter? Francis was not falling in love with another woman. He was in love with himself. He would love any woman who gave him assurance of that self.

"You're a very truthful woman, Jennet," she said. "I don't believe Francis can bear the truth—about himself, especially."

"What do you mean, Mother?"

"He felt you saw him as he is. Of course he doesn't know it."

"Mother, I love him!"

"Not as he is."

"But—but he could be so much!"

"He doesn't want to be."

"I only wanted to help him!"

"He doesn't want your help."

"I thought I ought—"

"It was no good." She drew her eyes from the

blank wall and forced herself to look at Jennet. She must compel herself to forget this was her child's face. Let it be the face of a woman—any woman, suffering.

"She—this girl—will probably help him more than you can, Jennet. She'll make him feel he has to—for her sake—because she's incompetent, helpless, whatever term you want to give general uselessness."

"Could I have—"

"You can't pretend, Jennet. You can't hide what you are. If you had tried it wouldn't have lasted." She could not deny herself the luxury of a secret bitterness that Jennet would not understand because she didn't know. "Ordinary men will just say that such women as you and I are managing—that we like to control—" Then she felt ashamed that she had stooped to bitterness. "That doesn't matter," she said. "You and I— we have to be what we are born. If we walk alone because of it we walk alone. Once in a while women like us do find someone—it must be there are some." Dr. Maclean's eyes moved back to the blank wall again. There was a long silence.

Then Jennet spoke. "I've got to think it over, by myself."

Her mother rose. "Yes, of course. I'll be back tonight." She permitted herself one step toward the bed and a quick hard kiss on Jennet's hand. "I'll telephone Francis that you know," she said clearly. In the same clear voice she went on, "Better not feed the baby tonight. I'll tell the nurse to bottle-feed her because you've had a shock—unavoidably."

"Thank you, Mother." Jennet's quiet voice denied her hard bright eyes, the spots of red upon her cheeks. Her mother paused an instant more.

"How I admire you!" she said. "I've never seen a woman take a blow as well."

They gazed at each other with desperate courage, each gauging the depths of the other's pain.

"You're a superior woman," Jennet's mother said with a sad smile. "There aren't many men able to let you be that, you know."

Jennet's lips quivered. "I don't want to be what Francis can't love," she whispered. She turned her head away and her mother refused herself the impulse to take that proud head in her arms. Jennet would not forgive her if she let her weep. She put her hand on the door.

"You have to be what you are born, my child," she said, and went away.

Nothing, Dr. Maclean thought to herself, would ever be hard for her again. She had told people that they must die because there was no cure for their illness. But even that would not be so hard after this. It would have been easier, she thought in the telephone booth, waiting for Francis to answer, if she had been able to say to Jennet simply, "He is dead."

"Hello, hello!" His voice was lively at her ear.

"Is that you, Francis? This is Jennet's mother."

"Oh—yes." The liveliness drained away.

"I just wanted to tell you that I have told Jennet. She will not expect you tonight."

"How is she?" The voice was uneasy at her ear.

"Jennet is brave enough for the truth, always."

"I know—but—"

"Tomorrow she will come to me. She will stay with me until she knows what to do."

"That's fine of you."

She disdained to answer this and she hung up the receiver. Now she must go home and tell Gareth.

"You mustn't be too hard on him," Gareth said. She had told him after dinner when they were alone together in the very room where Jennet had been married two years ago. She had told him that Jennet was coming home to live for a while. When he asked why she had in exactly the same gentle tone said that Francis had fallen in love with his secretary and Jennet must find out how serious it was. "A commonplace occurrence," she had added—thinking that she had allowed no bitterness to escape her. And then Gareth had spoken so quickly, more quickly than she had heard him speak for years, that she was startled.

"Am I hard?" she asked.

"You are judging him," he said. "I can feel it." He turned his head restlessly away from her. "All the right is on your side," he said. "So do not judge him."

"Tell me what you mean," she said. She leaned forward, aware of something about to be discovered which had been hidden from her all these years.

"He can't help it," Gareth said, not looking at her.

"No?"

"No. He has fought against loving this other woman. He wants to do what is right. But he knows that if he does what is right he faces years of complete blankness."

"With Jennet? How can that be?"

"You see—she's too big for him and he knows it. He is miserable because he knows it. She has given up too much for him."

"But it was such happiness for her to give up everything for him!" She was pleading with him.

"Yes, but it is impossible for her to forget that she has given up everything, and he knows it."

"She has never reminded him of it."

"He feels it. He asks himself over and over again if it was right for him to allow her to give up all that she could do in the world—for him."

"But darling, darling, she wanted to!" Her voice was a cry from her own youth.

"Yes, but had she the right to give up being what she really was? And besides—" His head dropped.

"Gareth, go on!"

"It changed her because she couldn't give up her true nature. Too much energy, too much power in her, applied to a small area. He wanted to get away from it. It was too much for him." His voice died away.

"So he went to war," she thought, "not as a doctor, even—as a private soldier, to escape from *me*."

"Is Jennet to blame?" she asked aloud.

He lifted his white head. "Oh no," he said

eagerly. "Not in the least—ever! How can she help what she is? But it would take a very strong man to—to be happy with her. Francis isn't—strong. He isn't strong enough even to be himself the way he used to be, the way he wants to be! It's all he can do just to exist!"

"I see," she said slowly. "Yes, you've made me see everything."

"Yes," he said. "Well—"

Her sore heart quivered upon new pain. "And is it true," she asked quietly, "that this other woman has helped Francis to know himself like this?"

His eyelids fluttered. "I—I think so."

"Will he come back to Jennet some day?"

He pondered this, frowning, and then asked her, "Will Jennet want him back?"

It was she who hesitated now. Oh, would Jennet want him back at such cost of loneliness and long silence, she being unalterably what she was, even as he? Did people ever change what they were? If she could have known when Gareth went to France long ago what he had now told her, would she have wanted him back to live the life they had lived so solitarily side by side in the same house?

"No," she said. She met for a moment a look in his eyes that terrified her, a look so knowing, so aware, so full of his old intelligence suddenly come to life.

"Gareth!" she cried. She fell on her knees before him and clasped him in her arms. Was he about to come back to her at last, his spirit returned to his body? "Dearest! Tell me who she was!"

Sweat broke out on his forehead. She felt a might straining in him, as though something were ready to burst from him. "Yes—yes," she whispered.

"I wanted—to forget."

"If you tell me, perhaps you can," she urged him. "It's so long ago, can't you tell me now?" It seemed to her that she must know, she had to know who was the woman Gareth had really loved and had left because he felt his duty to his wife. "Tell me, Gareth!" she cried.

He saw her face there, close to him, and he shivered and was still. Little by little the strength went out of him and the light drew back from his eyes. He could not speak. He had been silent too long. The years had made him what he now was. He looked at her vaguely with his accustomed look. She refused her loss.

"You aren't sorry you came home to me?" she pleaded.

"I?" All the old hesitation was back again. "No, of course not. No, of course I—wanted to come home."

"This has been home—here with me?"

"Yes, yes, of course, I couldn't think of any other."

Finer stuff, she thought, than Francis, better than Francis could ever be! He had come home to her, loyal to her, all his determination toward her, and then had escaped her as inevitably as though he had never come back. He had learned to endure sorrow by escaping from life, and that escape, first voluntary, had become involuntary, first conscious, it had become unconscious, until he became the shell of a man, his mind alive, his heart dead. Would she ever know why? No, for he did not know what he had done. He believed that he had come back to her. He did not know that he never had, because he could not.

"Better not to let him come back," she said to Jennet. It was night. The hospital was still, except that somewhere a woman was crying, somewhere a long way off. As long as she and Jennet talked they could not hear it. "It will never be the same, dear child. I know it."

"You—don't believe that men have to have escapades?"

"Not the sort of men for you and me, Jennet." She smiled wryly. "We aren't easy wives, perhaps, for ordinary men. We can't help that. We're women —first."

Jennet turned her head away. "I don't want him back."

"Then it will be easier."

"As long as I don't have to see him." She stared up at the ceiling. "Do I have to see him?"

"No, darling."

"Because I know I don't want him. If I saw him, I might—want him at any cost."

"Be very sure what you want."

"I am," Jennet said. "The cost would be, we'd both be miserable. Why should we both be if he can be happy with another woman?"

"And you? Think of yourself—a little."

"Can you think of any chance for me—except one?"

"Work," Dr. Maclean said.

"Work," Jennet agreed steadily.

"Back at the old stand?" John Benton caught up with her in the corridor.

"Back at the old stand," she said. He was a head above her tallness. It was not often a man was as tall as that. She had not remembered.

"We were both wrong about those slides," he said abruptly.

"Which?" She had forgotten.

"They were malignant—patient died," he said, without bothering to remind her. She remembered of her own accord.

"Oh that," she said. She looked at him and sighed. "You're two years ahead of me."

"I've kept pegging along," he said cheerfully.

"What have you taken up?"

"Heart," he said.

"Which is harder, heart or brain?" she asked.

"Nip and tuck," he said.

"I'm taking brain," she said.

They had reached the door of Dr. Farland's office. She nodded to John Benton and went in, exactly as she had two years—two years and six months ago. Dr. Farland was there at his desk, well again, or very nearly. There was a little twist to his left side. But his voice was almost as clear as ever.

"Well, Jennet?" Did she imagine his eyes avoided her? He busied himself with papers.

"Will you give me the same chance I had before, sir?"

"I'll give you anything in God's world I can, dear."

She fended off the warmth in his voice. She could bear anything these days but that. Only the love of two little girls could she bear now, and perhaps forever—if there were such a thing in the universe now as forever!

"Then I'll sign up for brain surgery again, sir. I'm going to specialize in brain."

"The hardest thing there is." He frowned. "Jennet, why do you choose the place where you'll find the greatest hardship for yourself? Prejudice and all that, besides?"

She meditated a whip. What if she said, "But I've been through prejudice and all that at home?" She put the whip aside. Whips were not for her. Little people used whips.

"I shan't mind, sir," she said.

He looked at her, admiration and tradition struggling together in his look. But most of the time he was an honest man and he let admiration win.

"I don't pretend to understand you," he grumbled, "any more than I've ever understood your mother. But—" He pulled a printed sheet of paper toward him and ran his pencil down its columns to a pause. "Here," he said. "Anatomy of the Brain—it's hours in the laboratory. Sure that's what you want?''

''Yes,'' she said.

He lifted his head at that full, onrushing voice.

''All right,'' he said, ''all right!''

She turned and marched out of the room, her head up. He watched her squared shoulders, aware of a curious disruption in certain old grooves of his being. Francis had missed something—he had missed some very big thing somewhere in this girl. He rubbed his hair in irritation.

''Damned if I'd want to marry her, though,'' he thought. Edith had made him a good wife. She was the sort of woman a man could forget entirely when he wasn't with her.

But outside the office door John Benton was still standing. Jennet found him there when she came out. He fell into step with her.

''Just waited to see whether old Farland would let you go on,'' he said. ''He's dead set against women around here.''

''He had to let me go on,'' she said. Then she lifted her brave dark eyes. ''How do you feel?''

''Feel?'' he repeated.

''About women being surgeons?''

''Oh that,'' he said, still drowned in those dark depths, ''oh, why not? Of course.''

She drew her eyes away and he breathed deeply. Relieved, that's what he was! In a moment more he would have been telling what he really felt and it wasn't time for that. It was much too soon, because he had only just realized himself what he was feeling.

"Damned if here isn't a woman I want to marry," he thought for the first time in his life.

The Two Women

SHE OPENED THE DOOR at the sound of a knock and there he stood. Three years they had been divorced and she never expected to see him again. Yet here he was on a cool spring evening, standing on the threshold of the house that had been theirs together and now for the three years had been hers. Lonely as a cave it had been until she got used to waking up in the morning in the silence and going to bed alone. "Watch yourself for the first year," her widowed mother had said before she died. "You'll marry anything to keep from sheer loneliness, but if you can weather the first year, you'll be used to it. Some day you'll like being alone."

She did not like it—not yet, but she was used to it and it was a shock to see him standing there on the doorstep, as handsome as ever, as she could see, the same dark handsome face that had wrenched the heart out of her bosom when she first saw him at her girl friend's house. She had made up her mind at once that she would have him, though she took him away from a girl who had been her friend since they went to kindergarten together. It was only five weeks to the day after their first meeting when they were married. "Too soon, too soon," her father had shouted when she told him. "Who knows what the fellow is?" When she had insisted he had growled at her that she could get a divorce if she didn't like the fellow, and she had replied that she was marrying Jacque Bronson for keeps.

"What have you come for now?" she asked him.

"I thought I'd come to see you," he said, half smiling, half pleading. He had a coaxing voice and tender eyes.

"There's nothing to see me about," she said. "I was just making a little dinner for myself. But come in."

"Thank you," he said and came in. He hung his hat on the hook behind the door where he used always to hang it and he went to the fire that was blazing in the smart modern chimneypiece in the corner and stood warming his hands.

"The air is chill tonight," he said.

He was heavier than he used to be, she noticed. He had aged more than the three years that had passed since he left this house, taking with him the things he wanted, his French books, the Picasso painting, the ivory chess set. The house was hers, left her by her own father so that in any case she would have a roof over her head, and he had fixed it so that she could never transfer the deed, though in her mad love she would have given everything away. She had wanted to belong to Jacque Bronson body and soul, with all her goods. But she was glad in the end that her father had left her the house and enough money, too, so that when Jacque had told her he was leaving for the love of another woman, she could say proudly that he need not think of her for she could look after herself. And she had done so, and simply enough after she had become chief editor in a large publishing house. Had there been children Jacque could not have left.

"No reason why you shouldn't have children," the doctor had said, "yet sometimes a normal man and woman just don't have a child—unconscious hostility for an unknown reason."

"Jacque and I love each other," she had declared.

The doctor had shrugged. "Well, then—"

Nevertheless, there had never been a child.

"I won't ask you to dinner, Jacque," she said now as she busied herself about the table. "Your wife will be expecting you home."

A mythical character, this wife, though she said the two words so smoothly, her voice matter of fact.

"What are you having?" he asked. He turned himself at the fire to warm his backside.

"I've made myself a little pot of beef stew," she said. "It's an easy way to cook for one—carrots and potatoes and meat and everything together."

She always laid the table meticulously, though only for herself, but tonight she took her best mats from the linen drawer in the chest of drawers that served as a buffet, one of the embroidered set that her mother had left her, and she chose a knife, fork and spoon from the old family silver that had come down from her English ancestry.

"I haven't eaten a stew like that since I left," he said. "Lilian isn't a cook."

She did not reply. It was nothing to her what Lilian was. She had never seen the woman and never intended to see her. The fragrance of the stew, now ready to eat, scented the air.

"Smells good," he said, sniffing.

She laughed suddenly. "You've not lost your old habit of hinting!"

He was relieved by her laughter. "I won't hint, then. Will you share your dinner with me, Stella?"

"I will not," she said firmly. "You belong at your home with her."

He made a slight grimace. "The truth is, we had a quarrel this morning and I told her I didn't know when I'd be back."

"You'll be back," she said. "I know those quarrels of yours. You get yourself in the mood for them. Especially in the spring after a long winter! Your mother told me before I married you that I was to look out for spring. You're the restless type, she told me. Spoiled by your mother, I say—and by me. Oh, you're spoiled!"

"And why should I want to quarrel with a woman?" he demanded. "It only leads to trouble. You're an unforgiving lot. Though it was Lilian that started it this morning, not me—"

She interrupted sharply, "Don't complain of your wife!"

He stepped toward her. "Look here, if you won't let me stay, I'll not go home anyway!"

They faced each other for an instant, he as bold and wilful as ever, and she as tempted.

"Very well," she said at last, "on the condition

that you call her and tell her you won't be home. It's only fair. I know what it was like when you didn't show up and didn't call!''

"Oh, all right," he said, and he went to the telephone on the small table by the door and dialed.

She walked away to the fire. She sat down on the green chair and tried not to listen and did listen.

"Hello, Lil? Just to tell you I'll not be home for dinner . . . Yes, I'm sorry. I hadn't planned—of course I'm in my office, where else? . . . I'm having a sandwich sent in. Of course I'm alone! . . . All right, I'll tell you what you want to hear—I am drunk, I'm in a tavern, I have a girl sitting on each knee! There now—aren't you happy? Better than the truth, isn't it?''

He gave a harsh bellow of laughter. "Take it or leave it, honey! Anyway, I'll be home in two hours sharp . . . All right—all right, eat it yourself or let it keep until tomorrow . . . I'm sorry . . . I said I'm sorry!''

He banged the receiver and came toward her. "She's the kind that gives a man no rope. She wants him to hang himself so that she can feel aggrieved.''

"You're not being fair to her, I'm sure," she said calmly.

"Maybe I'm not. But she's dull, Stella! Oh God! I should never—''

"She's pretty, isn't she?''

"Pretty isn't enough. I should never have—''

She rose. "Let's have our dinner. Then you must go home.''

She put the stew on the table and lit the candles.

"Don't make company of me," he said gruffly.

"Oh no," she said carelessly. "I light the candles every night."

"Because I used not to like candlelight?"

"Because I did, and do," she retorted.

She took the chair at the end of the table and served the stew. He would have been the one to serve it in the old days but now she was the head of her own house, and he sat at her right.

"Hot rolls under that napkin in the silver dish," she told him, "and help yourself to the salad. It's all I'd planned for dinner except some fruit and cheese."

"Suits me," he said. "I never like a lot of dishes, as you well know."

Now that they sat at the same table again, they were ill at ease. She knew he was doubtful of himself, neither husband nor guest, and she said nothing to reassure him. It was not good, this meeting, not at all good, and she must not let it happen again. She began to feel a distrust of herself. What was this stir in her blood? Was it possible that a part of her could still yearn for him? Or was it only that she had known no man for so long? She fortified herself. The past was still alive in her physical being, would always be alive, and her good acute mind must deliver her from evil. For evil it was to yield the flesh and not the spirit. Rebel flesh was recalcitrant and difficult enough but spirit outraged was shame and desolation.

"I don't like this at all," she said suddenly. "I don't want any part in your deceiving your wife."

"She was willing enough to deceive you," he said shortly.

"I'm not the same sort," she declared as shortly.

She knew at this instant that she could not finish the meal. The glowing fire, the warm room, the soft candlelight, the wooing of his dark eyes, the memories coming to life by his presence, all would be her undoing unless she put a stop to everything. She rose in resolution.

"I want you to go home at once, Jacque. Go home and tell her where you've been."

He put down his knife and fork. "You know very well what hell that will mean!"

"I do know—it was hell for me once!"

"Sit down while I tell you what I came to say," he commanded. "Sit down."

"I'd rather not," she insisted. But she leaned on the back of her chair, arms folded, and waited for him to speak.

"Listen to me," he said harshly, dark eyes burning into her eyes. "I was a fool to have married her. I should have had an affair with her and got her out of my system. She bores me to death now. You could make me angry, as you very well know, but you never bored me. Stella! I want to come back."

They gazed at each other, unflinching. She remained silent as long as she could.

"Why did you ever go?" she inquired at last.

He threw his napkin on the floor and came toward her, impetuous. She retreated, dragging the chair with her, keeping it between them.

"Oh no," she said breathlessly, "it's not as easy as that—you merely saying you want to come back! I asked you a question. You have it to answer."

He flushed red under his tan. "All right," he said. "I don't talk about sex as you very well know. I hate such talk. I'm the kind that does it with no talk, but if you must have talk! Before we were married—when we went to the doctor's office—to get our test, remember? He said to me privately that I wasn't to expect good sex from you. He said you were too—intelligent for a woman."

"And you believed him?"

"Sure I believed him! Wasn't he your family doctor? He got you born, didn't he?"

"That doesn't mean he knows me."

"As much him as anyone else—"

"You needn't have believed him."

"So far as my experience goes, he was right. So I—spared you."

"Spared me!"

"Yes! Did I ever force you? No! You called the tune and when it wasn't my tune I—"

"Had an affair with another woman," she said bitterly.

"I never said so," he retorted.

"Sparing me again, I suppose!"

"Exactly. I told myself you couldn't help being what you were born—a damned virginal brain!"

She flung the chair aside and walked away from him across the room to the chimneypiece. She mended the fire, thrust some kindling under the dying logs and set it ablaze with the small hand bellows. He stood watching her, gauging her mood, waiting. She knew what he was doing. When he made her angry enough, she was roused to anger and then to—response. The rush of the blood, the physical attack and then her yielding, he remembered and used as a weapon again. Ah, he was too confident, standing there gazing at her! She had learned how to live alone. She dusted her hands free of the bits of wood and turned to him, her head high and her cheeks hot.

"Go home, Jacque," she said. "Go home and prove to her that you are man enough to tell her what you've said to me."

His eyes narrowed as he stared at her. He opened his lips to say something and closed them again. Without a word he took his hat and coat and left her. And when he was gone she cleared the table, washed the dishes and put out the candles. Then seeing by the clock that it was the hour for her usual news broadcast she turned on the television. The familiar unknown face broke upon the screen.

"Invasion," the commentator was saying. "Unexpected and without cause, India is resisting, but it is questionable whether she can withstand the—''

She turned a button and face and voice disappeared. Invasion! It was here in her own house.

In the morning, while she lingered over her coffee, the sun shining callously cheerful as ever, she lifted her eyes and caught by accident the sight of her face in the long mirror over her dressing table and opposite her bed. She was an early riser, a morning worker, but this morning she had no inclination to rise or to work. A pile of manuscripts lay on her desk. This was her reading day, the day she did not go to the office, a day she enjoyed for its quiet and its detachment. It would not be fair to read manuscripts now, however, her brain murky with sleeplessness and conflict. Instead she had pattered barefoot to the kitchen, had made coffee and returned to bed. And now here she was staring at the drawn face in the mirror.

"You," she muttered between set teeth, "you fool, wanting him back in this bed with you!"

And furious, it occurred to her to think of Lilian, who had taken him from her. Their positions were strangely reversed. It was Lilian who was the wife now and she, Stella, was the other woman. How she had longed to meet Lilian face to face and see for herself what sort of woman had bewitched Jacque away from his wife! For they had been happily married, she had believed, and now her belief was confirmed by his wish to return. But Lilian had not been willing to meet her.

"She's shy," Jacque had explained. "She's afraid of you. She thinks you have brains."

"Do you mean this Lilian has no brains of her own?" she had demanded.

Jacque had twisted his lips into a new sort of smile. "Maybe not," he had conceded, "you wouldn't call what she has brains, but—"

He had shrugged and she had looked away, repelled and silenced. Now, remembering, she made up her mind that she would go to Lilian, just as once she had wished Lilian would come to her. She rose on the impulse and showered and dressed in a feverish haste. If she saw Lilian face to face, if they talked, if she explained that she had not known Jacque was coming last night, then all would be honest and she could be bold. She could ask straightly,

"Do you think—"

Here she paused, gloved and hatted and her little sable scarf about the neck of her new green suit. Suddenly she knew that it was she who was afraid. Suppose Lilian would not give him up? Then they would simply have to battle it out and let the best woman win. She stopped a cab and in a quarter of an hour was at the house. A decorous maid answered the doorbell and ushered her into a square living room and even as she entered she saw a young woman enter from another door.

"I am Stella," she said, and put out her hand. "And you are Lilian."

"It's too silly we haven't met," Lilian replied and laughed a tinkle of mirth.

"It is silly," Stella agreed.

"Do sit down."

They were in the living room of the new house he had bought when he married Lilian, a room surprisingly pleasant. She had expected to find something overdecorated and feminine. Instead it was a sensible room, designed for a man's physical comfort, the chair large and deep, the sofa long and ample, the pictures good. Nor did Lilian look out of place in this room of solid furniture and simply curtained windows. It was an old house, the walls thick and the sills deep. She did not know that Jacque liked an old house. Impatient and modern, she had always taken it for granted that he would oppose the traditional, yet here was tradition. Even the woman for whom he had left her was somehow traditional, her softly knotted light brown hair natural and straight, her face pretty with fine fair skin and dark blue eyes. She wore a blue tailored blouse and a skirt of blue tweed, and no jewelry, and she had an honest womanly face, even the prettiness wholesome and not what she thought would have attracted Jacque. And yet she thought she knew him, those wary secret dark eyes of his, always roving in the direction of the dashing and the young. Instead here was this soft-voiced woman, this soft, round-faced female!

"I've always wanted to know what you were like," Lilian was saying. "I thought it would help me to understand Jacque better. But you aren't a bit what I thought you'd be."

Stella smiled. "What did you think I was?"

Lilian blushed. "I should be ashamed, but I thought you'd be different—"

"Perhaps I am differrent," Stella said gently, "although it all depends on different from what."

"Of course I know you are clever and intellectual and all that," Lilian went on, "but I thought you'd be very voguish and—extreme. You're slim, but not as thin as I thought. I'm always fighting fat and I supposed you—"

"I hope he doesn't bully you."

"Oh no, he doesn't like skinny women, he says, but then you're not skinny—not really."

She stared at Stella with naive wide eyes, baby blue. "I don't know that I like your looking the way you do," she blurted.

"Forgive me," Stella said in the same gentle voice.

Inwardly she was trying to recover from shock. How could it be possible that Jacque, subtle and impenetrable, young and old at the same time, spoiled by his European childhood and his French mother, how could he have left her for this! And yet, she understood.

There was something refreshing here, uncomplicated, uncritical, easygoing, undemanding. Surely she herself had never been critical of him, stimulating, yes, but not critical! She could hear her own voice.

"You've a fine mind, Jacque. When you let yourself think, you're worth listening to—"

His response had been strange, uncomfortable laughter, uneasy and yet relishing her praise. He needed praise. He sought it and yet he rejected it, was hungry for it and denied its sustenance.

"You can't help it," Lilian was saying.

"Can't help?"

"Looking the way you do. Tell me—"

She pulled a hassock close to Stella's chair and sitting upon it leaned her chin on her clenched hands. "Tell me, did he used to sit for hours and say nothing— nothing at all?"

How could she tell this sweet woman that Jacque never sat silent for long and never, never said nothing at all? The trouble was that she and he exhausted themselves with talking. Not business, they had decided. She with her editorial job and he the executive in an advertising firm could assemble so formidable an agenda for lively conversation, each doing research, as he put it, through the other's brain, that when at last they went to bed they were often too tired for sleep—or for love.

"We destroyed each other," she thought.

"Why doesn't he talk?" Lilian was asking.

"Perhaps he likes to listen to you," she said.

"He doesn't hear me."

"How do you know?"

"I ask him a question, on purpose, and he doesn't know how to answer because he hasn't been listening."

"He has an exacting job. It demands constant alertness. Perhaps it's silence he needs."

"I wish he wouldn't bring so much work home at night."

Ah, but that was what they had agreed, that they would never bring work home at night, not she from her office and not he from his! The nights were to be their own.

"Lately it's been two and three in the morning before he comes to bed," Lilian was saying. "He doesn't even wake me. Then in the morning he sleeps until it's late and he has to rush."

"He's always slept late and rushed," Stella said.

Then she saw Lilian's face, the eyes filling, the tender childlike mouth. Her hands dropped and she began folding a pleat in her skirt.

"I'm afraid he—I think he's in love with someone else. He came home last night in a terrible mood. He scarcely spoke to me when we went to bed."

Stella made her voice very dry. "As a matter of fact, he stopped in to see me. I was surprised. I hadn't seen him since the divorce."

"Oh—" The word was a faint cry.

Now was the time to speak, speak now or forever

be silent—wasn't that what the marriage ceremony said?

"Did he say anything about me?" Lilian's voice was a half whisper.

How answer this demand? Lie? This was no time for lying. Truth? Truth was weighted, depending upon the heart that must bear it. Truth was for her, not Lilian. Truth was to ask once and for all, did she want him back? Yes, her heart said. I want him back. At all costs? At all costs, except—

She turned her head away. At the window she saw the yellow gold of a forsythia bush, breaking into bloom in the small walled garden at the back of the house.

"Do you like flowers?" she asked.

Lilian drew back surprised, wary. "Of course—don't you?"

"I don't know. I've never had time to grow them. I've worked ever since I left college. Of course I buy them for decoration. But that's not like growing them—one has them for a few days and throws them away when they die. Do you intend to have children?"

"Oh yes, oh yes—as soon as he's willing."

"Why not now?"

"He says—"

"Don't pay attention to what he says. Go on and have a child."

"Why didn't you—"

"No time—or I thought not—and then—suddenly it was too late."

"Too late?"

"He was in love with you. What was the use of a child to break my heart again?"

"Oh, don't!" Lilian put her hands over her ears. Then she dropped them. "But he told me you didn't love him. He said he was starved. He said you —you—"

She looked at Lilian. "I suppose he said I didn't understand him."

"How did you know?"

She shrugged, she smoothed her grey kid gloves on her knee. "It's the usual complaint, isn't it?"

"You mean you do understand him?"

"In my way. Do you?"

"I don't know. He thinks—he thinks now that I don't."

"You do," she said flatly. "In your way."

Without meaning to, without knowing it, she realized she had struck upon the truth.

"Such a pity," she murmured.

"What?"

"That we weren't one woman—I with your body, for example, and you with my—"

"Brains?"

She could not inflict the hurt. "Something of me," she admitted, "the something you don't have. Between us we might have been enough for him."

They sat for a long moment in silence, two women, both loving the one man. It was Stella who broke the silence.

"My advice," she said, "is that you have a child.

Don't ask him when or if. Simply have one! I suppose you—''

She lifted her eyebrows. Absurd that she could not go on and say, I suppose that you are all right in bed? But the words would not be spoken. They stabbed her with longing. It would be so easy, now that they had met last night, he and she, now that he, briefly discontented, wanted to come back to her. It would be so easy to let it all slide into the routine of love, the sharp delightful conflict between their complementing minds, the mutual stimulation of thought against thought, ending as it so often did in the total of union. For they never really quarrelled. The contrast there was between the two of them was conflict enough.

''Oh yes, thank God,'' Lilian was saying eagerly and without shame. ''At least I can give him that. It's what I tell myself. I'm so humble, really. I'm quite often afraid I'm stupid. But it doesn't matter, I tell myself, if he is satisfied with me as a woman.''

As a woman! Stella bit back words of triumph. ''Ah, but you see he isn't satisfied with you as a woman! If he had been he'd never have come back to me last night.''

Then she'd see this pink and white creature shrivel. Then she'd walk out of this house as the conqueror—to do what? What would she do when he came to accuse her and to hate her for what she had done to Lilian? So what was the use of triumph?

She rose, she drew on the grey kid gloves. Then upon an impulse she took the pink and white face, the pretty girlish face, between her two grey kid palms.

"Oh, God," she said softly. "What does a man want? Only everything! And between us, my dear, we must give it to him. Have your baby. And if once in a while he stops by my house to talk, to complain, to argue, to—to—whatever he happens to want to do, don't worry. I'll keep him in your bounds, my dear. You can trust me. You'll be safer with me than with some other woman who doesn't know him as I do—or as I know you, now that I've seen you."

She let her hands drop and then felt a soft kiss on her cheek, a kiss she did not want but there it was. She left the house quickly and looked back only once. Lilian was at the window, her face above the yellow forsythia flowers, a puzzled face but very pretty. Had Lilian understood a word of all that talk? Probably not, but she was glad she had put it into words, for herself. She'd not take him back, or only just enough to make him content to be faithful to his wife. Ah, that was the primary loyalty between women, the only loyalty that mattered, if the world were not to lose its balance! And then, having settled three lives into place again and thus prepared for the birth of a child, she walked briskly toward a waiting taxicab and stepped inside.

"Take me to my office," she said. "At the corner of Fifty-seventh and Fifth Avenue."

Miranda

ROGER BRACE WAS READY to fall in love. He had decided when he finished college that he would not marry until he had finished medical school, and when he had finished medical school that he would wait until he had ended his internship. At that point, since he had guarded his heart so well he decided that he would establish himself in practice and earn ten thousand dollars a year before he considered being in love with intent to marry. That moment had now come. His combination secretary and receptionist, a pretty girl, had a few minutes ago brought to his desk his income tax returns for the first quarter of the year, and he was startled to see the size of the check he must sign.

"Good God," he exclaimed. "This means that I am earning over ten thousand a year!"

"At least that, Dr. Brace," she had replied with a smile.

He took up his pen with a strange feeling about his heart. Shackles dropped somewhere in that region of his being, although he felt not so much a new freedom as a sensation of collapsing walls. There was nothing now to protect him, while he searched for the woman with whom he could fall in love. He enjoyed women when they were young and pretty, but he had always protected himself against them. Sooner or later he said gently, "I am not free yet to think of marriage." It had not been necessary to explain what this freedom was. It was quite enough to murmur the few words, for then the expanding female flower, the pretty face with the yearning eyes, the coaxing voice, shrank away like a sensitive plant. Or as in the case of Miranda, pride flamed to the roots of her dark hair. Miranda had made firm and quick retort.

"A woman doctor should never marry."

"Why not?" he had demanded.

"Any woman can get married," she had said insolently.

That was not true but he had not said so. Miranda had probably had proposals, yet he knew as a medical fact that there were women, nice, even rather pretty women, who had never had a proposal. He knew because they were often his patients, and it was his duty as a doctor to diagnose their illness. It was simply that no man asked them in marriage. This diagnosis must of course be kept secret. It would never do to say to a young woman nearing her thirties, certainly not if she were in her forties, that what she needed was marriage. Instead he had to prescribe rest or change of activity or a new interest, and, as a sop, powders and pills. Subtly indeed the balance of human life was being changed. In Japan, for example, where he had done his military service, there were four women to every man. Even a white man was a prize, under those circumstances. And here in the United States, a paradise for women, he had always supposed, he was often aware of an uncomfortable feeling of being pursued. Yes, although he avoided statistics in his own environment, he knew very well that as a man he was no longer the pursuer but the pursued.

Ten thousand a year! The figures provided his fate. There was now no reason whatever against his falling in love and marrying the woman he loved, if and when he could find her. Marriage might indeed be the permanent protection he needed. Instead of saying, "I am not yet free to marry," it might be even safer to say, "I am already married." But he must not marry in haste.

His secretary was standing there waiting for his signature.

"Sorry, Miss Branson."

He scrawled his name hastily.

"Not at all, Dr. Brace," she murmured.

She smiled at him and went away, the check fluttering in her neat fingers. There was a nice girl, he thought, very nice, and ready to fall in love. He had warded off as a matter of course, and even absent-mindedly, her glances, her devotion to duty, her habit of the red rose upon his desk, fresh every morning. He guessed that she took the rose home with her at night, kept it on her own table, doubtless, and made it a rite to buy the fresh one the next day. He sighed. Poor girl, and poor girls everywhere, not because of him—he blushed slightly, for he was naturally a decently modest man and he hoped that he was not a fool—but merely because women ought to marry and so often could not.

He pressed the buzzer on his desk for his office nurse, and heard her voice, a deep and troubling contralto.

"Yes, Dr. Brace?"

"I am ready for my first patient."

"Yes, Dr. Brace."

In a moment the door opened and she came in, a beautiful sultry-looking girl and he could never understand why she was only a trained nurse. She had a voice that could shake the soul, warm and thrilling. He had heard her sing sometimes when she thought she was alone in the laboratory, blues of Louisiana, where she had come from, and once he had told her that she was wasted here in his office.

"You ought to be in Hollywood, my child," he said.

"I'm no child, Dr. Brace." She had lifted dark eyes to his and startled him enough so that he had instantly left the room.

She stood before him now, her white uniform immaculate. The belt she girdled about her waist was incredibly small in contrast to the round and slender hips and the full bosom. "Your first patient is Miss Anita Romberg. Don't let her knock you off your feet."

He laughed. "Don't worry, Sally!"

"I'm jealous," she murmured.

He ignored this and she repeated it. "I'm jealous enough to die."

"All right, Sally," he said abruptly. "This is a busy day."

She gave him a long look, disappeared and came back with a beautiful blonde girl in a white serge suit and a white ermine stole. She was small and very slight and her eyes were the purest blue he had ever seen. He was alarmed by such beauty and immediately went cold. "Sit down, please, Miss Romberg," he said.

She sat down, the stole slid to the floor. Sally picked it up, touching it tenderly.

"Oh, thank you," Miss Romberg said in a silvery voice.

"All right, Sally," he said pointedly. Behind Miss Romberg's back Sally blew him a brazen kiss and went away.

"Now, Miss Romberg," he said coldly. "Will you describe your symptoms?"

He was glancing rapidly over the record sheet. Twenty-five, an actress, sleepless, loss of energy, malaise, no appetite.

She leaned forward, her face suddenly wistful. "I know what's the matter with me, Dr. Brace. I'm disappointed in love."

"That seems impossible," he said politely.

"It's true," she insisted. "I'm desperately in love with a married man. That's not sensible, is it?"

He disliked the conversation intensely. "It depends on circumstances," he said.

She shrugged her right shoulder. "The circumstances are so ordinary they aren't worth mentioning. He's married to a rich wife, and he doesn't want to divorce her. That leaves me just—out."

"Suppose we discuss your physical symptoms," he suggested.

She threw out a pair of prettily gloved and very small hands. "I can't eat, I can't sleep. I'm not working well. I have to cure myself somehow. I've tried psychiatry. It's no good—I'm not inhibited. I thought if you gave me something just to make me sleep and make me want to eat, I could get on my feet again.''

"I can do that," he said, "but suppose we make an examination, as a precaution.''

He buzzed and Sally came in. "Prepare Miss Romberg, please," he ordered.

The two women went out together and he sat thinking over the case. There was really no cure except time, and even time would provide no permanent cure unless it also provided love. That was what she needed, simple old-fashioned love.

"Ready, Dr. Brace," Sally said. He got up and went into the next room and made his usual careful examination. Heart was sound, vital organs all in good shape, tonsils small and clean, eyes, ears and nose quite perfect, teeth admirable, all the muscular reactions excellent. He said nothing and went back to his desk.

"I can't find anything wrong, Miss Romberg," he said when she came back, dressed again.

"I told you," she murmured.

"I'll give you a tonic," he said, and looking up inadvertently he was startled again by her beauty.

"Pity," he said calmly. "Why don't you have an affair and get it out of your system?"

She shrugged her shoulder again. "As though that were a cure for love! It's the real thing, unfortunately.''

"Not with him?"

"He's too cautious. Men are fearfully cautious, aren't they?"

"We have to be," he said.

"I suppose so," she said reasonably.

She went away then, his prescription tucked into her glove, and he buzzed for Sally. "Next case," he said.

At the end of the day whose cases were distressingly alike, he felt the need to consult. What doctor could be more suitable than Miranda Saunders, herself a woman? Yet she was not as other women. She was dedicated to her profession and they could talk in the clear cold atmosphere of science, although applied to entirely unscientific and emotional human beings.

He buzzed for his secretary.

"Call Dr. Miranda Saunders and ask her if she will dine with me tonight. I want to have some shop talk."

"Yes, sir," the girl murmured.

He took his next case and when he returned to his desk, he found a note there.

"Dr. Saunders will meet you at the Porcelain Pagoda at seven—"

At five minutes past seven he met Miranda at the restaurant door. She looked very cool and handsome in a suit of pearl grey and a wide cerise hat, dashingly becoming to her dark hair and eyes and her white skin.

They shook hands briskly and she led the way in and chose the table and they sat down.

"I've ordered our dinner," she said. "The food is better if one does. What's this shop talk?"

He wished for once that she were not so brusque,

so forthright. She had a beautiful mouth, the lips full and sculptured, and tonight she had put on lipstick, for the cerise hat, he supposed. Anyway, she was unexpectedly stunning. But he outlined the case of Miss Romberg.

"It is dishonest," he said at last. "It is quite dishonest of me to keep prescribing pills and powders for women whose trouble is simple enough. They have a biological function to perform and the mores of our society are such that they cannot perform them. They are compelled to a partial life, in a physiological sense."

Miranda contradicted him in a pleasantly scientific fashion. "It is not entirely physiological. Biologic, perhaps but not even quite—well, only if you include in the biologic the complete cycle of love and mating and reproduction. I am not sure, however, whether our society has not warped this trinity into something wholly unrealistic. That is, love is overstressed, and mating is merely romantic fulfillment, while reproduction may be accidental or even unwelcome. What we have is a female who is egocentric, and this is unnatural. She thinks in terms of her own love needs, herself the be-all and end-all. Women must be re-educated again to their primary function."

He looked at her with admiration. He had seen her often enough in her surgical garments, for she was a surgeon and a good one, so that she numbered as many men as women among her patients. Her face was actually appealing in a feminine way under her wide hat, and she had drawn off her gloves. Her hands were well shaped and she had tinted the nails, a sight he had never seen before.

A waiter brought four hot dishes on a tray and placed them symmetrically on the table. "I'll serve," Miranda said.

Roger watched her hands, capable and strong, at their task.

"Merely scientifically," he said, "how is it that you have educated your own biological nature so well? I believe you told me that you never intend to marry."

He was surprised to see her blush quite thoroughly. "How like a man to be personal," she replied. "I might ask you the same question, but I won't. I don't consider it my business."

"If you did ask me," he said daringly, "I would answer you honestly. I am ready to fall in love and to marry. My income nicely tops ten thousand a year and it will increase. There is no reason now why I shouldn't fulfill any function I wish."

She looked uninterested, choosing an olive from a dish of olives and cracked ice. She ate it before she replied. "What a pity you can only solve the problem for one woman! The Chinese, now, are so clever. Let's ask Miss Jade Purity over there how it's done in her country. She and I are good friends. When I'm alone here she often sits down at my table and drinks tea with me."

She waved her hand toward a charming slender young Chinese girl who hovered at a distance, and the girl came forward all in smiles.

"Jade Purity," Miranda said, "please sit down. Don't be afraid of my friend, although he is a man. He is exceedingly well behaved. As two physicians, we have been discussing the problem of our patients who are women. He tells me that he is ashamed to go on prescribing pills and powders for young women who are only ill because they cannot find husbands, or at least the husbands they want. Miss Jade Purity, Dr. Brace."

Miss Jade Purity sat down with obvious pleasure. She was a small dainty woman, married to the manager of the restaurant, and she had four children whom she left with her mother-in-law in the rooms behind the restaurant while she kept an eye on the waitresses and the cashbox. Like most Chinese women of good class, she used her own name after her marriage. Besides, she looked too young to be married.

"I can agree with you, Dr. Brace," she said in lively and inaccurate English. "American girls have too much responsibility. They are so worried from husband hunting. Then suppose the one they wish is not asking them, what can they do? Nothing! If they are brassy, they ask him and he is shocked and doesn't like. If they are not brassy they wait and wait some more, maybe forever. Maybe taking some leftovers or snatching married man somewhere."

"Exactly," he said. "You have put it very succinctly. What concerns me as a physician is that they are often ill in the process, or later when they give up hope.''

"What do you suggest, Jade Purity?" Miranda asked. Her eyes were humorous under their dark lashes.

The small matron raised narrow black eyebrows, painted carefully above her somewhat round eyes, and she shrugged her shoulders which were fitted tightly into a mauve silk Chinese gown.

"How to suggest!" she mused. "I can only say my own case. I took no responsibility myself. It was not my duty. My parents brought me into the world, it is their duty to provide my husband. I am only carefree all my life. In high school I am seeing the American girls so anxious for dates, etcetera. I am not anxious. Why should I want dates? My parents will do it. When I am finished high school my father said, 'Your mother and I are thinking three young men are good husbands for you. Here are their pictures, not fancy but true. This is number one good, this is number two better, this is number three best.' He shows me pictures, and naturally I choose number three, who is my husband yonder, getting a little fat, but he is still very good. I choose him, he chooses me under parents' wishing, and so we are quite happy, certainly at present. I am a good wife also, I must say. We are making quite a lot of money and our children will go to college. I am satisfied.''

Miss Jade Purity did indeed look entirely satisfied. She was calm, she was cheerful, and she took pride in her pretty face and slim figure, as well as in her husband and children. Roger Brace looked at her with admiration. She was carefree and even debonair because she had been fundamentally provided for. But then she was a Chinese woman and she did not expect much, not Clark Gable for example, or not even perhaps a lover. She had a good man and she was fond of him.

"Thank you, Jade Purity," Miranda said.

Miss Jade Purity rose. "Any time you want to ask me something, please do so," she said smartly and walked away.

Roger laughed. "I shall start a new school of thought," he declared. "I shall begin to educate my patients. I shall tell my young women to demand that their parents provide husbands for them."

"And you," Miranda said with a wry smile, "would you be willing to practice what you prescribe? Isn't there something somewhere about a physician healing himself?"

"Oh, I shall marry," he said cheerfully. "The point now is to fall in love."

She lifted her eyes to his again, disconcertingly clear. "Why fall in love?" she asked. "I'm sure Jade Purity didn't mean that."

He stared back at her. "But we want to fall in love, we Americans—don't we?"

"Speak for yourself—I have no wish to fall in love," she said in the coolest voice he had ever heard.

There might have been no more to it then except that within five minutes the accident occurred. Every accident is also a coincidence, and this one was no exception. Miss Jade Purity had returned to the cashier's desk, and her husband, who was deeply in love with her in a comfortable way, sauntered toward her and leaned on the ledge outside the window.

"Something wrong with the order over there?" he asked in Chinese.

Miss Jade Purity counted dollar bills and rolled them into little bundles. "Nothing," she replied. "They are talking about marriage."

"Then why did they talk with you?" he inquired. He was a man of small incessant curiosities, and she enjoyed satisfying him.

"They say many American women are getting sick because they cannot find husbands for themselves and I told them how much better is our way. Certainly I took no trouble to find you, and yet you are very nice."

He laughed fondly. One of her most pleasant traits was her desire to please him. He returned her compliments. "I tell you, I was smart enough to see that you were the best one out of the five pictures my parents showed to me."

She teased him. "Five? Last time you said only four."

"Maybe six," he retorted.

They both laughed in the mild foolish fashion of two people who like each other, although they are married. He stepped back and at this moment collided with Roger, who had approached to pay the bill. The shock was severe. Mr. Chang was short but heavy, and Roger, taller by a foot and slim as an athlete, was the one to lose his balance. Mr. Chang merely grunted and stood still until he saw Roger, wavering, fall to one knee on the tiled floor.

"Oh, excuse me," Mr. Chang cried in much distress. He tried to lift the American, but Roger was in a trance of pain.

"It's my knee," he gasped. "I crushed it once in football, and it's never been entirely right. I've damaged it again, I'm afraid—"

"Lean on me," Miranda said. She bent and slipped his right arm over her shoulders, and Mr. Chang quickly took his place on Roger's left.

"We'll get a taxi," Miranda said, "and I'll take you straight to the hospital."

"I hate—to—to spoil your evening," Roger muttered. His face was greenish pale with exquisite pain, and he felt actually giddy.

"Nonsense," she said, beckoning a taxicab. "Now get in, Roger."

"I haven't paid the check," he murmured.

"No money, please," Mr. Chang declared in great distress. "I am an ox, so clumsy!"

"Nonsense," Miranda said, "the dinner was delicious." She took the money from Roger's hand and forced it on Mr. Chang, and left him standing on the curb, looking anxious.

"Now," Miranda said. "I'm going to examine your knee myself—X-ray it."

"I warn you," Roger said faintly. "I am a good doctor but a very bad patient."

"I am just a good doctor," Miranda said with surprising conceit.

She was excellent, he could not deny it. She examined his knee under X-ray and by touch, and she made a diagnosis with which he could not disagree. "A slight operation," she decided, "removing what I believe will be splintered bone fragments of a previous blow—and released again by your fall—"

He woke up from ether in a daze of relaxation. His knee was bandaged comfortably and his leg suspended just enough to relieve him of its weight. He gazed into Miranda's face and smiled and was instantly aware of something in her observing eyes which gave him alarm, something warm and verging on tenderness. He was in danger. This was no time to fall in love, not while he was on his back and helpless. He did not want any maternalism mixed up in his marriage, no mothering, if you please! But her voice was quite cold.

"You can get up in a few days," she said, "whenever you like, in fact. You know enough to watch your own symptoms."

"Just let me be a patient for once, will you? It feels good." Then he added a mischievous thought. "And send me a pretty nurse!"

She laughed suddenly. "I have a very pretty nurse, and I'll detach her for you. She's on a tiresome case just now, an old and fussy woman. She needs a change to a handsome young man. It'll be a vacation for her."

"Wonderful," he murmured.

He fell asleep and when he woke the pretty nurse was there, a fabulously pretty nurse, he decided, more so than Sally. She was small and red-haired and her eyes were as green as grass.

"Hi," she said, and came to his bedside and stood looking down at him with frankly delighted eyes.

"Hello," he said, "I'm thirsty."

She went away and came back with a glass of ice cold orange juice.

"I snitched it for you," she said in a whisper, "when the head nurse wasn't looking."

"You're a nurse after my own heart," he said and drank the glass empty in a breath.

"Oh my," she said, "I hope you don't regret that."

"I shan't," he promised.

He felt well indeed, rested and relieved of responsibilities.

"It was nice of Dr. Miranda Saunders to keep her promise so quickly," he said.

"Did she promise you something?" the pretty nurse asked.

"You," he said, "And what's your name?"

"Lily," she said, "Lily Burns."

"Tiger Lily," he suggested.

"How did you know they call me that?" she asked, surprised.

"Honey, you don't look like just a lily," he said.

"I'm not," she agreed. She threw him a look—oh, the same look that he knew so well, the free gift that any girl gives to a young and handsome man, especially a blue-eyed blonde young giant who used to play football in college.

"It's a shame about your knee," she said softly.

"My knee is going to be better than it has been since I was a freshman," he said.

"Oh, Dr. Saunders is a wonderful surgeon," the Tiger Lily said. "Everybody knows that."

Something in her voice suggested a question. "Just a surgeon, eh?" he asked.

The Tiger Lily pouted a childishly pretty mouth. "Well, she can't be everything, can she?"

"Meaning that a surgeon is not necessarily an attractive woman?"

"Oh, she's attractive—isn't she?"

"I think so," he said.

"If you like the type," she said.

Ah ha, he thought, little claws! "See here," he said. "She sent you to take care of me. She isn't jealous, at least."

The Tiger Lily flushed. "And that I don't call natural," she cried. "It stands to reason—"

She stopped.

"What reason, little one?" he asked.

"A girl has to look out for herself," the Tiger Lily said.

The reply stopped instantly his mood of playfulness. "I suppose so," he said in a wary voice.

"She has to," the Tiger Lily repeated passionately, "because if she doesn't, who will?"

"Nobody," he agreed. He closed his eyes. "I'm tired, I think. Draw the shade, will you? I'm going to sleep."

"Yes, sir," the pretty nurse said. "Shall I go away?"

"If you will, please," he said, quite as a command.

She went away and he was alone again, but he was not at all sleepy. He was, as a matter of fact, only tired of women, very tired. They had to look out for themselves.

He was cool after that for fully twenty-four hours. The next morning he sent for his secretary and dictated letters and signed checks. After all, he told Miranda, when she made her usual morning call, there was nothing the matter with his brain.

"Much better to keep busy," she agreed.

He warded off a hint of emotion from his secretary. No, he didn't want a red rose here, he didn't like flowers in a hospital room. She could keep it. And no, he didn't know just when he would be back in the office. He might as well take a few days of vacation while he had the excuse. Miss Romberg had called four times? Tell her he was not seeing anyone after a surgical operation. And Sally could have some days off if she wanted them.

No, he did not want her here to nurse him—they'd just talk shop. He didn't want anybody he knew around him. Yes, he realized how they all felt, he appreciated being missed and he missed everybody, but he needed a little vacation, nevertheless.

The lovely girl went away with tears in her eyes because she had never seen Dr. Brace so cross and she was sure that something more was wrong than just his knee.

In the afternoon, still conscience-smitten, Mr. Chang came to see him with a package of fresh almond cakes which the chef had just baked. He presented them with a wide smile.

"Almond cakes must be so fresh if good," he explained. "Usually they are not so fresh and they are not good. These are fresh and good, still somewhat hot."

"Thank you," Roger said. "They smell heavenly."

Mr. Chang laughed and sat down carefully on the edge of a chair and put on a sorrowful face. "How is your knee today?" he asked.

"Very well indeed," Roger said. "The operation was entirely successful."

"Good," Mr. Chang said. "Still I am not forgiving myself."

"Please," Roger said, "you are really my benefactor. You made me have the operation which I knew I needed anyway. I'd put it off for years."

Mr. Chang beamed. "Fate, not me," he declared. "Everything is fate."

"You think so?" Roger asked. "Now that's very interesting. Do you think it was fate, for example, that you and Miss Jade Purity became husband and wife? Was it not arranged by your parents?"

"Certainly only fate," Mr. Chang replied without hesitation. "Parents naturally choose several who are suitable girls for me. In fact, seven. But fate decides which of the seven, possible eight, is the right one. Why Jade Purity you may ask? Two or possible three are more beautiful. Four or possible five are also good cooks. Jade Purity! Well, why? Something I like there, that's all. It is fate. Entirely seven or eight girls, possible nine even, are all good enough, and parents protect me so much so I don't hurry somewhere and fall in love, naturally. Parents choose so many girls good enough, but fate tells me the one I like best. Then I fall in love safely."

Mr. Chang laughed and wiped away a dew of perspiration from his somewhat oily skin.

These last words were an illumination. "You fell in love safely, eh?" Roger repeated.

"Quite safe," Mr. Chang said. "Very comfortable, I may say. Otherwise dangerous for me, because so many girls everywhere and wishing to fall in love is so dangerous."

"Dangerous," Roger repeated.

"Yes," the voluble Mr. Chang said, "too dangerous for any man! Wishing to fall in love at falling in love age, any man falls in love with any pretty girl. But safe falling in love is not dangerous."

"Explain," Roger begged.

Mr. Chang ticked off explanations on his surprisingly long and slender fingers. "One, she must be interest in what I am interest, as for example, restaurant. Two, she must be faithful and good also. Three, she must like how I like. Four, she must not be lazy. Five, she must not be selfish. Six, she must not be jealous, if some nice-looking lady customer comes in, for example, and I must be polite. Seven, liking babies very much. Eight, polite to husband and his parents. Nine—"

"Wait," Roger said, "I'll have to get those by heart."

Mr. Chang opened his little eyes. "Are you looking for wife?"

"More or less," Roger said.

Mr. Chang drew in his breath loudly. "Ah ha, Jade Purity says so! She told lady doctor she thinks so, and she hopes very much two doctors will marry. That will be safe falling in love."

"You think so?" Roger inquired earnestly.

"Oh, very," Mr. Chang said with decision. "One, because lady doctor is interest in your interest. Two, she is also very faithful and good. Three—"

"Wait," Roger said. "What did the lady doctor say?"

"She says she is not looking for husband, thank you."

"Oh!" Roger felt let down.

"Never mind," Mr. Chang said for comfort.

"Plenty more, you know. Such handsome man like you, many girls are wanting."

He got up to go. "I must not to stay too long. But I hope you are well."

"Wait," Roger said, "one more question. Suppose you had wanted Miss Jade Purity and she had not wanted you? Suppose she had chosen one of the others?"

"What others?" Mr. Chang asked innocently.

"She told us that her parents showed her the pictures of three young men."

Mr. Chang laughed heartily. "I think they were not three. I think at most one other, and maybe in fact, no other at all, only me. We cannot tell. Young girls are liking to think of many men. But she agreed to me and I am also her fate. We are quite satisfied together. Goodbye, Dr. Brace, and asking you to forgive me."

"Goodbye," Roger said, "and I thank you instead of forgiving you."

He was alone again and when the Tiger Lily put her head in the door he snapped at her cruelly. "I don't want anything—"

"Oh my," she said. "We're cross today, aren't we!"

She shut the door and he was alone. So, he thought grimly, Miranda wasn't looking for a husband! She was the wonderful exception, was she, the great independent woman, who didn't need a man to help her or look after her or—or even love her! He felt hurt and then he felt angry. Was there something the matter with him, pray? Was he cross-eyed or hunchbacked or did he have halitosis? This was a nice thing for a man to hear, that he had been suggested to a woman as a husband and she had turned him down, even before he had proposed! It was insulting, that was what it was, and he did not intend to take it. If he loved a woman, it was his right to propose to her himself and hear from her own lips why he was impossible, obnoxious, repulsive.

He lay working himself up and by the time Miranda came in for her evening call, he was in a bad temper.

"There is no reason why you can't go home tomorrow." That was what she said when she came in.

"You want to get rid of me, eh?" he demanded.

He was so vehement that she looked surprised. "We are always crowded, and you don't need hospitalization any longer. Your nurse reports that you are restless, that you have no fever and that you are eating well. A few days with a crutch—"

"I shan't walk on a crutch," he declared. "I shall stay here until I am ready to go."

He was pleased to see that she was not as handsome as usual. She looked tired, her dark hair was slipping down, and she wore no lipstick. A hard day, probably, but it was her own choice to be a surgeon instead of marrying some fine man and letting him take care of her—

"Why, Roger Brace," she said, "I don't know what to make of you!" She sat down in a chair and for the first time since he had known her, she looked surprised and helpless. He sat up in bed.

"Miranda, how dared you tell that Chinese girl that you didn't want me for a husband?"

She stared at him and then blushed so brilliantly that her paleness was instantly gone and her dark eyes sparkled. "I don't," she said.

"Why not?" he demanded.

"Aside from the fact that I am not thinking of marriage, as I have told you over and over again—"

"Yes, and why not?" he demanded. "You're a woman, aren't you?"

Unexpectedly, unknowingly, he had pierced her heart. She drooped her head and hesitated. Then she said in her honest and quiet way, "Yes, I am, and that's my curse."

He was too astonished to retaliate. Her beautiful face, all agony and shyness, her eyelashes resting on her flushed cheeks, her lovely mouth—

"Miranda!" he whispered.

She did not move.

"Miranda, come here!" he commanded.

She shook her drooping head. He felt the blood rush to his heart and it began to beat like a tom-tom drum against his ribs. "Miranda, I'm falling in love with you—" he muttered.

He felt very strange indeed. A yearning ache in his breast was distinctly uncomfortable and he was not sure he liked it.

She lifted her head, startled, and the flush faded

from her face, leaving her very white. "It's impossible—"

"It's true, I tell you. I feel queer enough to—maybe it's fate, as Mr. Chang said."

"Roger, be sensible. I hate joking on such subjects." She stood up and looked at him severely.

"Miranda, I am not joking. Come here! Or shall I have to get out of bed in my pajamas?"

"Oh, Roger—" she laughed. "You're being silly—"

But she went to his side, half reluctantly, and he seized her hands.

"Miranda, if I can feel like this when you're looking your worst—"

She snatched her right hand away and put it to her hair—"I've had three operations this afternoon—"

"Darling, I guessed it. It's too much. I ought to be up and looking after you. I'm getting up tomorrow. Three is too much for any surgeon, and you can't go on like this. I forbid it!"

She sank down on the bed and bent her head over their clasped hands.

"I really don't want to get married, Roger. I mean it. I love my work—"

"Of course, darling, why not? Keep on loving it, will you? I'll enjoy being jealous of it. It'll keep me on my toes. And I like your fingernails without paint and your lips without lipstick—and oh, Miranda, I feel so safe falling in love with you! Please, please darling, feel safe to fall in love with me? Can you, do you think?"

He laid his cheek on her dark disordered hair and kissed her ear.

"Oh, I don't know," she murmured distracted. "It's nothing I planned—"

"Of course not," he agreed. "That's why it's fate. You can't plan your fate, it just happens that way. Lift up your head, darling—isn't it so?"

He slipped his hand under her chin. Oh, what a soft sweet chin to be so firm, and she lifted her head at that and looked at him, eyes dewy and lips quivering, her face all sensitive and alive and shy and bewildered at once.

"Isn't it so, Miranda?" he insisted.

"Oh Roger," she said, half laughing, half crying.

"Yes, Roger," he commanded. "Say it—"

"I—can't just—"

He was compelled to kiss her, of course, just to prove to her that he could. It was a long kiss, masterfully held on his part as long as breath allowed.

"Now," he began again when they drew apart, quite dazed. "Isn't it so, Miranda?"

"Yes, Roger," she said.

"Yes, Roger, what?" he demanded.

"It's fate," she said.

The Kiss

BERT RANDALL LOOKED at his watch. It was seven forty-five, the moment at which he left the house every day for his office. Thirteen minutes took him to the train and he allowed three minutes in which to put on his hat and overcoat and kiss his wife goodbye.

"Well—" he said, breaking off. He threw down his napkin and got up and walked with his usual firm step the length of the table.

"Goodbye, Jenny," he said. Her name was Jennifer but he considered it fancy, and as soon as they were married he had begun to call her Jenny.

"Goodbye, dear," she said. She was a handsome woman, with dark composed eyes and a brown skin. Her hair was black and her tall figure was broad-shouldered, thin and elegant. She put down her coffee cup and turned her cheek. He had bent his head and then delayed unexpectedly.

"Hey, how about a real kiss?" he demanded.

He took her chin in his large smooth hand and tilted her face and kissed her soundly on the lips.

"A nice coffee-flavored kiss," she said.

Laughter rumbled in his belly. "Ungrateful woman," he said.

She watched him reflectively through the wide picture window a moment later. He was a big good-looking man, too heavy, but there was nothing she could do about that except in silent protest to keep herself as slender as a girl. That kiss! It was his idea, she supposed, of being subtle, as if she didn't know what it meant!

She poured a second cup of coffee. This was the hour of the day which she liked best of all, when there was no one in the house but herself. She liked her house, a pleasant one, larger than they could afford when they had bought it, but which he had managed because she wanted it. Now that he could afford it she toyed with the idea of adding a wing, a music room for herself and some sort of a room for him, call it a library, perhaps, except that he did not read very much. He could call it what he liked.

That kiss! It was still on her lips, distasteful at this time of the morning. But she had never liked to be kissed, and for that he could not be blamed. Even as a child, when she was compelled to kiss her parents before she went upstairs to bed, it had been each night a momentary ordeal. She had always suppressed her aversion for she loved her father and mother quite normally, or perhaps in the modern vernacular, she did not hate them as much as she was supposed to. Indeed she could not remember that she had hated them at all. Nevertheless, it had been repulsive to touch her lips to theirs, for she could not keep from thinking how they looked when they were putting food into their mouths. Sometimes when she sat between them at the table, a too thoughtful child, she would watch her mother nibble her toast in small buttered bits and her father's big white teeth champing down on beefsteak and potatoes. That, she would think, is what I have to kiss tonight. Even her baby brother's small wet mouth she did not like upon her lips or face. He was the demonstrative child, the affectionate one, and yet she had loved them all in her silent way. It's quite physical, she thought. It has nothing to do with loving. Saliva is disgusting. It is as simple as that.

She sipped her black coffee slowly and felt ashamed of herself. Bert was the best husband in the world and she loved him. She had no interest in any other man and never would have and she could not understand those Kinsey Report women who had affairs with other men—the indelicacy! And why, when it was now proved that women were not like men, did they want affairs? It was a great comfort to discover that women really were not like men, and so there was nothing wrong with her simply because she did not want to sleep with Bert every night. Hemingway! Those women he wrote about—always ready to snuggle into a sleeping bag with a man! Not that she cared if they enjoyed it, but it was nice to know that he had simply made them up out of his own imagination or—still and all, why did she now remember that one kiss, long ago, the one she refused to give? Of all the kisses she had given and received the one she had refused was the only one she still wondered about, and remembered, with a strange sad longing.

Yet would I, she thought, have remembered it so clearly, at least this morning, unless I had read in the paper yesterday that Rae Lancaster was opening tonight in a Broadway musical show?

Still, it was not only this morning. In the autumn, a season which always made her vaguely sad, she was given to looking back and pondering upon what she could regret, and then she always thought of the kiss she had not given—or received. It might have been something quite different, it might indeed have changed the whole course of her life. She might never have met Bert. And yet it was long ago, when she was only a girl, and she had been an ugly girl, rawboned and gawky and her face all features. Through high school she had been hopeless and no boy had ever looked at her. She had pretended she did not care but she did in a way, not really, perhaps, because inside she was happy enough, and had liked school and she was already beginning to be mad about music then, and nobody mattered in particular except that she liked parties and to get to a dance you had to have a boy so she went to no dances. Then she had gone to a girls' college for two years and not knowing any boys from high school there was no chance then either, and so she had first met the tall young Englishman, who was studying at Juilliard where she had decided to go instead of finishing college. He was there for voice and she for piano. He had a fine tenor and she played his accompaniments, at first because her professor had suggested it, and then because she played the way he liked. They were both hard workers, concentrating upon their music and not thinking of each other. Still, he was the first man she had ever been with for hours on end alone, and it was inevitable that she did sometimes think about him, or perhaps only feel him there, a presence different from her own. He was exaggeratedly tall, fair hair, a high English nose and very blue eyes, a delicately shaped mouth for a man and his hands were always hot; that she remembered even now. His voice was beautiful, but clear and cold, in spite of his charming impetuous manners.

And suddenly one day without an instant's warning when he had finished singing he had leaned over her as her hands came to rest on the ivory keys and he had said,

"Give me a kiss, will you?"

Like that! She had never kissed any boy, not even in games, because of hating kissing and now to her wonder, she wanted to kiss him. As suddenly as he had spoken the desire to kiss him came hot to her lips. Why not? Only—well, the habit of a lifetime, even of a short one, is not so easily broken. And she had added to it some romantic notion, partly her mother's teaching, partly her own defense because no boy had ever pursued her, that she would never kiss a man unless they were in love.

She had looked away, had taken the music sheets from the piano and put them carefully together.

"I'm not that sort of a girl," she had said in a low voice.

"What sort of a girl?" he had asked, still leaning toward her.

"That sort," she had repeated dizzily, "to kiss—without loving."

He did not reply. He kept silent, looking at her, as she could feel, and she looked back at him, a darting discerning look, and saw in his blue eyes a simple yearning. "And you," she said bitterly, "you don't love me, either."

"I want to kiss you," he pleaded.

"No!" she had said strongly to this.

Instead of reply he coughed slightly behind his hand and fumbled with his music. "Do you mind," he said, "if we try the last page and a half over again?"

They had gone on working for another three quarters of an hour and then they had parted exactly as usual and the kiss was not mentioned again. The semester was nearly over, as a matter of fact, and in less than two weeks he went back to England and she had never seen him or heard of him until yesterday.

And what, she mused here alone at her breakfast table, what would have happened if she had kissed him? Would they then have loved? Perhaps she had been quite wrong. Perhaps love came after the first kiss, and not before, the kiss being the test, the touchstone, the spark that lit the tinder. Well, it was too late to know. When Bert proposed he did not kiss her until she had accepted him, and it was an awkward kiss for them both. Now, of course, she could discern exactly what Bert's kisses meant. Sometimes mere duty, or habit, sometimes affectionate thanks, sometimes warning.

She glanced involuntarily at her watch. Ten

o'clock—the ticket office would be open and she could settle the matter of the kiss. She would get a ticket for a matinee, so that she could go alone and look at him and listen to him. Then she would know whether she had been right or wrong. And no sooner had she decided this than the telephone rang and it was Bert, saying that he could not get home early after all. An out-of-town client had come in with a tax problem, and he'd have to spend the evening.

"Then I shall go to the theater by myself and pick you up later," she said.

It was nothing new, she had often done exactly the same thing before, and they always met at the garage where she left the car.

"I'm sorry, Jenny," Bert said. "I wanted to get home early tonight."

"Oh well," she said, "we'll come home together."

She hung up and stood frowning slightly and thinking. Why not simply do the bold thing and call Rae Lancaster herself and tell him that she wanted a ticket for the opening tonight? The theater was a sellout, that the newspaper had declared, but there were always house tickets. He could get one for her if he wanted to, and if he didn't want to, then she need not go. The question would be settled.

She took up the telephone again and after arguing with three people, a man and two women, secretaries, agents, whatever it was he surrounded himself with these days, she heard his voice, older, more confident, but still gay and sentimental. Yes, as she remembered it, he had a sentimental voice.

"Do you remember Jennifer Bruelle?" she asked.

He did not hesitate. "Of course! You did my first accompaniments. Where are you?"

"At home. Look, I don't want to bother you, but I want a ticket for tonight."

"Just one?"

She hesitated and then answered with hardihood. "Yes, I shall be alone."

"But of course there'll be a ticket for you, Jennifer," he said. "It will be at the ticket office—your name on it. I wish I could be there too, but you'll come backstage, won't you? We might have a little supper together—no, I forgot—something's planned. But I'll take you with me."

"Are you alone, too?" she asked, but it was not really lying, this pretending at being alone.

"Absolutely," he said frankly. "In fact, I've never been more alone. Don't you read the papers?"

"Not the English ones."

"Ah well, perhaps divorce is too common in this land of the free!"

"I mustn't keep you," she said to this.

"I'll see you tonight," he said.

So easily done! The day slipped by because she clung to the hours with a sense of fear. What risk was she taking, she a happily married woman who had no care in the world except this silly regret? She would go and see the play but she would not go backstage. She

would leave the theater quietly and alone and meet Bert
as she had said she would and never again would she
think about the kiss.

She dressed herself soberly in a black frock and her
pearls and drove herself to the city and put the car in the
garage. She had decided against dinner alone, and so
she was early at the theater, and only a few other people
were there. Her seat was the best, a middle place in the
fifth row, near enough to see and not too near to lose the
music. Bert did not care for music and she often came
alone to concerts and musicals. There was nothing
unusual in what she was doing except that she knew she
had never done such a thing before. She had never come
with the intent of meeting a man. Yes, she had the
intent, if—no use lying to herself! She would never
have dreamed of such a thing if she had not refused the
kiss. If she had yielded, certainly she would not be here.
She had not the slightest feeling for Rae, then or now.
The only question was, if she had yielded, would love
have exploded in her heart? They were so much alike,
he and she. That would have been a marriage entirely
different from the one she had made with Bert.

She sat half musing, half watching the people
come in, and before she knew it the curtain went up and
the orchestra began the new music, and then she stopped
thinking to hear it. It was queer dissonant stuff, catchy
too, but ugly almost to harshness. How would he sing
it? His voice had been pure and true, and this music kept
slipping into quarter tones. The stage was suddenly full
of people, confused brilliant display of color resolving

itself into a dance design. She almost forgot why she had come until the crowd receded and left the stage open, and he came in, walking on as casually as though he walked into her living room. He has not changed at all, she thought amazed, he is even wearing the same clothes, which of course could not be true but they sat on his thin tall figure with the same ease, a grey tweed and a black tie, and his fair hair was the same color. Then he began to sing and his voice was changed, deepened, enriched by use. Oh, he sang beautifully, that was sure, and he took the twisted music and difficult rhythm and sang it all clear, every tone and note with the same pure quality.

He saw her, she thought, but she was not sure, and she fastened her eyes on his face and listened, tense and stirred. Of course she would go backstage. It would be folly to miss the chance again.

"Miss Bruelle?"

"Here," she said quietly from the crowd waiting at his door.

A small excited man drew her aside and whispered. "Mr. Lancaster says, will you please wait a few minutes? He'll get rid of the others."

"Very well," she said. She sat down on a wooden chair. The door opened and the people went on in and she sat in a strange numbness, frightened at herself. She felt reckless, hypnotized perhaps by his singing, so that whatever he asked she would do. She would never be self-righteous again as long as she lived. But how would she ever tell Bert? And this then was how good and decent and respectable women began their affairs, out of a memory, out of a vague childhood repulsion! She understood the other women now, and humbly she knew that she was no better than they, respectable wives though they were, and as she had always been, for that matter. But if he asked her to kiss him, as he might, as he must, then this time she would not refuse. She looked down at her hands clasped in her lap and suddenly she took off her rings and dropped them in her bag.

"Come in, please, Miss Bruelle," the little man said in his excited voice.

She rose and went in and Rae Lancaster was standing there waiting for her. He shut the door and took her hand and stared at her.

"You haven't changed," he said warmly.

"You haven't, either," she said. She felt suddenly shy because he was so little changed, the same mobile youthful face and the bright blue eyes. He was incurably young, she thought, and yet things had happened to him, success, marriage, divorce.

"Sit down," he said, still clinging to her hand. "Sit down there on the couch. Let me look at you."

She sat down, her pale face flushing.

He looked at the left hand he held, and did not say the words. No rings? Since he did not ask she need not answer. She pulled her hand away gently.

"You sang gloriously," she said.

"Oh yes," he said carelessly, "I can sing. It's all I can do."

"You don't need to do anything else," she said.

"No," he agreed almost listlessly. "It keeps me busy. The voice is at its best just now. I have to make my hay."

He was the same discontented boy, she thought, always wanting something he did not have.

"You've been happy?" she asked gently.

"I suppose so," he said. "I shouldn't have married though—I'm not the marrying kind, it seems."

"I'm sorry," she said.

"Why aren't you married?" he asked.

To lie or not to lie! She felt the old wilful charm as strong as ever. He could never have taken care of her as Bert had done and delighted to do. She would have had to take care of him, but that might have been sweet. She had never taken care of anyone, not even a child.

"Let's not talk about me," she said. "I've done nothing interesting. I've just lived along."

"You're much more handsome than you used to be," he said suddenly. "I never used to think you were handsome but there was something about you, so quiet and steady and sure inside. You still are."

"Am I?"

"Not like me."

She sat quietly gazing at him, her hands folded in her lap and did not answer. She was feeling him through and through, a lost and lonely creature, she thought, not at all the easy self-confident boy who had walked out upon the stage.

He asked suddenly in the midst of her silence. "Do you remember I asked you to kiss me?"

"Yes," she said.

"Ah!" He threw her a shrewd and mischievous look. "You remember! And do you remember you refused?"

"Yes."

He laughed. "Oh, you never could tell a lie!" He clasped his hands over his knees and rocked back and forth laughing. Then with instant gaiety he leaned toward her.

"Give it to me now, Jennifer!"

She hesitated, fascinated and repelled.

"You've owed it to me," he insisted. "All these years—a debt!"

She shook her head. "Not a debt."

"Yes, it is," he insisted. "When a man invites a woman to a kiss, she owes it to him."

He leaned to her and let his charm creep into her veins and run like fire through her flesh. Let it be, she thought—and then she felt his lips press down upon hers in the kiss she had refused and then had never forgotten. They clung together for a long moment, and then he drew away.

"There," he said, smiling at her with a queer cold tenderness. "That was good. Now you can forget and so can I. Are you coming with me to my supper party?"

He rose, her hand in his, and he pulled her slightly, only enough to suggest that it was over. Then he saw her eyes.

"What is it?" he asked. "What have I done?"

"Do you remember what I said—when I refused?"

"You mean long ago?"

"Yes."

"I only remember that you refused me," he said.

"Then I will remind you," she said. "I will remind you of why I refused. I told you that we did not love each other."

"Well?" His voice was wondering and he did not evade her direct dark look.

"I was right to refuse you," she said. "The reason holds. Now that we have kissed, I know that the reason holds. It is a sin to kiss without love."

He had no comprehension of what she meant. She could see the honest wonder in his blue eyes, the puzzlement, his matter-of-course agreement.

"All right, dear," he said reasonably. "You didn't expect me to love you, did you?"

"No," she said, and was surprised that she meant it. She neither expected it nor wanted it. "It's late," she said, glancing at her watch. "I have another engagement." Should she tell him now that she was married? No, she would not, because he might think she was not happily married and she was, oh very much so, and she knew it at last.

"Good night," she said, smiling at him for the first

time with responding gaiety. "I'm glad we met again."

"Even glad for the kiss?"

"Oh yes," she said, "especially for that—because now I shall forget all about it."

She went away without looking at him and caught a cab and alone in the darkness she found her rings in her bag and put them on. When she reached the garage Bert was there already waiting for her and she hurried toward him.

"Oh, I hope you haven't waited long!"

"Only ten minutes or so," he said. "Just long enough to get the car out. Have a good time?"

"It was an unusual sort of play," she said.

They were in the car, he driving and she beside him, and they moved out into the quiet street and stopped a moment later for a red light, the only car at this late hour. She felt him looking at her and she turned to meet his eyes.

"Got a kiss for me, Jenny?"

"Oh yes," she said instantly.

She kissed him eagerly and sweetly, pressing her lips on his, accepting the morning's warning gladly. Why not? He loved her. So why not? This was the real kiss, and the other one was wafted away, as though it had never been.

The Man
Called Dead

DRAKE FORRESTER WOKE on Monday morning with more than his usual reluctance. On Saturdays and Sundays his agent closed his office and for two days he knew he could not ask the question or receive the answer. The question was always the same, and so was the answer.

"Have you heard of anything, Nick?"

"No, Drake, sorry, not yet, I have all sorts of lines out, as I told you, but no fish."

The next two sentences were likewise always the same.

"Thanks, Nick. If there is the slightest chance—"

"I know, I know, old man. I'd be on your doorstep in five minutes."

There might or might not follow the next hesitating words.

"Had I better tell you where I'll be today?"

"No, no, it's not that close, old man."

He was never anywhere but in his one-room apartment in this third-rate apartment house, unless he went out for a walk or a cheap meal somewhere. He was finished, he was through, the early promise had never been fulfilled, the parts he had played so brilliantly, almost up to the lead in the last play, had not led anywhere. He was not too old yet, barely forty-five, but the big chance had never come. He had made the most of opportunity, but the lead part, the humorous, sophisticated, delightful part that he knew he could do was simply not popular any more. Playwrights weren't interested. They wrote about raw brutal lustful boys. That he was not and that he could not be. He was born out of his time, too late or too early. The civilizing influence of the old world was gone and the new American civilization had not yet arrived, that was how he excused himself. There was no place for him.

It was fortunate indeed that he had never married, that he and Sara had agreed to wait. Then she had married another man, someone he did not know. He did not blame her, five years was too long to wait, and there was nothing in prospect, even then. Years ago that was, twelve years and three months and two days. He had not even seen her picture in the papers since her husband died two years, four months and six days ago, and he did not write to her.

He got up unwillingly and went to the door for the morning paper. The moment of greatest comfort in his dreary day was when he crept back into his still warm bed with the morning paper. This morning his bed was an especial refuge. It was raining, he saw, as he shut the window against the raw spring air. At least he had the shelter of this room, this bed, and he had been wise enough so that he would not starve. One meal a day and the meager rent were assured. There was no particular joy in the barren security, but it meant that he could be indifferent about getting up and going out on a bad day.

He piled the two thin pillows under the wall bed-light, opened the paper, turned to the theater page and read it closely and thoroughly. No news there. The season's plays were probably settled by now and his only chance was with the summer playhouse. He must talk with Nick about that and urge him, Nick was getting careless, the old bonds of friendship and past success were wearing down. Yet he dared not go to another agent, if indeed one would take him on. Nick knew him, at least. He did not have to explain what he could do.

At this moment the bedlight, always uneasy upon the plaster wall, chose to fall from its hook. He threw down the paper in sudden anger and sprang up to set it back, when he saw his name leap at him from the scattered pages.

Drake Forrester Found Dead In His Apartment

It was a small headline on the back page. He seized the paper and took it to the window, and read his own obituary. ''Drake Forrester, an actor, was found dead in his bed this morning by an elevator man, who brought him his usual morning paper. Mr. Forrester was well known in former years in successful Broadway plays. He received offers from Hollywood which he did not accept, preferring to remain on the legitimate stage. In recent years—''

The paper fell from his hand. He rushed to the telephone to call up Nick. This had to be contradicted immediately, Nick must send out a press release, he would sue the newspaper.

A nasal voice replied, ''Nicholas Jansen Agency.''

"Oh yes," he said, stammering as he always did when he was upset. "Is Mr. Jansen in?

"Mr. Jansen won't be in today."

"Oh—do you know where he can be reached?"

"He can't be reached. He is spending the weekend in the country with an important client."

"Oh—"

He hesitated and then not knowing what else to say to the cold voice he muttered thanks and hung up and after another moment he went back to bed, covered himself up and shut his eyes. The paper fell on the floor and he gave himself up to loneliness.

Who cared whether it was true or not? Nobody had cared for a long time. His sister he had not heard from in years. She was married and lived in Texas. His parents had died when he was in his twenties, thank God, at the time it had seemed he would inevitably be famous. The theater was wickedly consuming, one had no life outside it, family and friends had fallen away.

He might as well be dead.

It was a strange feeling this being dead. Though he breathed and was awake in this room where he had lived so long, he was dead. His dramatic mind began to stir. He had read stories, he had even once seen a play on this very situation, and the man who was called dead had begun a new and completely free life, all the old debts cancelled, the failures erased. He might so welcome his freedom, he might do something entirely new, even take a new name and disappear from all he had known. He saw himself roaming about the world, a different person in one city or another, London, Paris, Venice, or even just Chicago or San Francisco.

There was no difficulty. He did not want to do anything except theater. Whatever else he attempted it would all end in a room like this somewhere, an agent trying to find him a job, and would an agent even try to find an unknown man a job? At least Drake Forrester had been somebody once, there was a memory.

It had been a long time since he had wept, but he wept now, only a few tears and not exactly for himself, but for anybody like him anywhere. He was not unique, of course. There was no use fooling himself. He had a little flair, a tiny talent that, combined with youth and extreme good looks—oh, he had been good-looking, still was—enough to carry him a little beyond the average, but it had not been enough and would never be enough for more than that.

So why not die? It would be easy, he had thought of it as anyone alone and unsuccessful thinks of it, not as something he would ever do, but still a possibility. He had thought of it sometimes at night when he took his sleeping pills. He held death in the palm of his hand, he had mused, gazing down on the white pellets, not with any reality in his mind, but with his little flair for drama, thinking that if he should so choose, he could do it.

Now someone else had done it for him, someone with his name. He took up the paper and read again. No reason was given for his death. It was simply announced with the few details about his former success on the stage and his gradual retirement. It was quite dignified, and if he died now, actually, the effect would be spoiled. This shabby room, his continual hounding of Nick, the ragged shirts and torn pajamas, the disgusting private details which he could keep hidden while he lived, but dead he must reveal. He ought really to be grateful that someone had died so nicely in his place. They had the address right, this street, this house.

He grinned, his lips twisted, and suddenly he felt hungry. He would get up, he would make his coffee and toast over the gas ring and he would never call Nick up again. He might leave here, he might go west tomorrow, saunter into Hollywood, later, quite on his own, and get any kind of a job around the sets, even a janitor's job. Nothing mattered, since his name was dead.

While he was drinking his coffee at his bedside table, the telephone rang suddenly. He got up and went to it. An unknown voice, a woman's voice, cried out, "Who is this, please?"

His name flew to his tongue and he checked it. "Whom do you want?" he growled.

"I've just seen the paper. I used to know Drake Forrester, years ago. We were in the same cast of a play. He was a good actor and I've often wondered—and now he's dead!"

He hesitated and then he said firmly, in the same deep voice, "Sorry, Madame, you have the wrong number." He hung up and sat down on his bed. But it was wonderful, nevertheless. Who could she have been? He was a good actor, she had not forgotten. He sat staring at the blank wall, trying to place the voice, and not being able to. Well, one person remembered. He felt cheered by so much and looked out of the window to see if it was still raining. On clear mornings he usually took a walk down the street.

It was still raining and he went back to bed and had scarcely settled himself when he heard a knock on the door. He got up again and opened it and there stood the janitor, looking surly and holding a small box of flowers.

"Oh, thanks," Drake said. "Wait a minute."

He went to his trousers hung over the chair and took out a dime. "Thanks a lot," he said.

The door shut and he opened the box of flowers. They were white roses and snapdragons with asparagus fern. There was an envelope and in it a card, "In memory of a swell time" the card said, and under it were signed seven names. He remembered them, people who had had bit parts in *The Red Circle*, the year it was almost a hit. It had been a mystery play, and he was the husband of the murdered woman, but the lead was the lover, not the husband. Still the run had been good and he had saved his money, thinking still that he and Sara would be married. That was the year she had married Harrison Page. It did not matter now. If he had been successful he would probably have been married to someone.

He put the flowers into the tin wastepaper basket, half filled it with water and set it in the window. He decided not to go back to bed, but to get up and go out. It was April and the sky was beginning to clear. He took a shower in the bathroom down the hall and came back and dressed carefully, and by the time he reached the street the clouds were white and ragged and scraps of blue sky were showing.

He took his usual walk around six blocks and since nobody knew him by name nobody was surprised to see him. He bought a copy of a small theatrical magazine, wondered if it were too cold yet to sit on a park bench and read, and decided it was and went back to his room. Not to call Nick gave him nothing at all to do, but he had made up his mind. He was not going to call Nick. When he felt like it he would consider further the question of where he would go, and maybe he would not go anywhere.

When he reached his room an envelope was stuck under his door, a telegram. He picked it up, tore it open and saw it was from Nick, a frantic appeal. "For God's sake, call me up. Been trying to get you for hours. Took the first train to town."

He sat down, his hat still on his head. Did this mean Nick knew he was dead or did not? Probably he had seen the news and did not believe it. Or maybe he thought someone was with him, he had never revealed to Nick the way he lived, and Nick supposed he had a mistress. Nick knew he had some money but he did not know how little. He decided again not to call Nick up. Without taking his hat off he put the telegram beside the flowers and went out again.

Back on the park bench, he read the magazine from cover to cover. Then he sat awhile looking thoughtfully about at other men on the park benches. He recognized several of them, and he supposed they recognized him but they had never spoken to each other and there was no reason why they should do so now. It was about noon and he decided that he would get some lunch in an automat nearby and then go back to his room and sleep. He felt tired with the uncertainty of his emotions. It was an experience to be dead, he thought, and grinned again to himself.

When he went into the old apartment house the janitor came shambling out. "Must be your birthday or something," he said. "Two more boxes of flowers come while you was gone, and three telegrams."

"It's an anniversary," Drake said. He fumbled for another dime and gave it to the janitor and loaded himself with the boxes, put the telegrams in his pocket and went upstairs. This was getting funny, his room full of flowers and telegrams. It was like being back in the theater in his dressing room. Congratulations on being dead!

But he was touched, for all that. He had thought himself completely forgotten, and now he knew he was not. He opened the flowers and put them into the tin wastepaper basket with the others, pale yellow roses and white spirea from the director of his first play, and spring flowers from the star in *The Red Circle*, the lover who murdered the wife. The telegrams were from members of the casts of his other plays and from a girl who used to work in Nick's office, who he knew well enough had once dreamed about him, only in those days he was still getting over Sara. The card was handwritten, ''In fondest memory, Louise.'' But he had always called her Miss Silverstein.

The room looked festive and cheerful. He had not made the bed, often he did not make it, but just got into it again the way he had left it, but now he made it carefully and found an old handkerchief and dusted the table, the window sill and the bureau. After some thought he took the yellow roses and spirea and put them in a milk bottle and set them on the bureau.

Then the telephone began to ring and kept on ringing until either he had to go out again or answer it. He took up the receiver cautiously.

''Hello,'' he said in a voice not at all like his own. But it was not Nick. It was a woman and her voice was gentle.

''Hello, is this where Drake Forrester used to live?''

''It is,'' he answered. Then he recognized the voice. His heart gave a fierce leap. It was Sara! She had the loveliest voice he had ever heard.

''I have only just read the dreadful news,'' the gentle voice said. ''Will you tell me where the services are to be? I used to know him years ago. I loved him very much, and I still do, though now I can never tell him.''

He could not speak. What could he say? Then silly words burst from him. ''Why didn't you tell him?''

She was surprised. ''Are you his friend?''

''In a way. He told me about you.''

"Oh, did he—he didn't forget?"

"Never!"

He was shocked at what was going on. He was weaving a new web, entangling himself beyond rescue.

"Oh, would you come and tell me about him?" she pleaded.

"Where are you?"

She gave him a street number far uptown, a long journey from where he stood. "I don't know just when—" So he began.

"Oh, come now," she begged. "I must know everything. Then I can explain to you why—you see, I lost him, I mean, after my husband died I didn't know where to turn. Besides, I never saw his name anywhere until this morning, and then I knew really that I meant all along to find him. I suppose I just kept dreaming."

"I'll come," he promised. He hung up the receiver. Though he had committed himself, he might yet break his promise, but he knew where she was and sooner or later, however much he delayed, he knew as he knew himself that he would be on her threshold, ringing the bell, waiting for the moment of her recognition. He had to come back to life.

The telephone was ringing and on the chance that it might be her again he took it up impulsively and was caught. "Hello!" he cried too eagerly.

It was Nick, exasperated. "Well, of all the goddamned nonsense! Where have you been all morning? I knew you weren't dead."

"How did you know it?" he demanded. He felt injured. Did Nick think he hadn't the courage—

"For a while I thought maybe it was true, you old fake," Nick said. "Then I read the news item again and saw it couldn't be you. They had you sixty-five—didn't you notice?"

"No," Drake said.

"You never could remember figgers," Nick said impatiently. "They had you born in 1887. I knew you wasn't born then. I've done too much publicity for you. I've been busy all morning. The newspaper is going to correct the error tomorrow. Seems some fellow down in Virginia had your name and the newspaper mixed him up with you and used your obituary from the files. Well, it's done you a lot of good anyway. I've got you a part."

"A part?"

"Yeah, a good one, not starring, but a solid part. New play, *South Side of the Moon*, looks good too. Summer tryouts, of course, then probably Broadway. Producer says he used to know you, he called me up to tell me he was sorry he hadn't kept up with you, says he could of used you, if he'd known, so I said to give me a few minutes. You come right up here, Drake, and I'll have the contract ready. We'll sew things up. I'm not going to let any grass grow, not from now on."

Drake wavered. He could not be in two places at once. Either he went to Sara first, or he went to Nick first. The decision was close, he was always an actor, and he had not for a long time been a lover. Could the old role be revived? His dramatic imagination leaped ahead. He saw himself in Sara's hall, or perhaps in her living room, waiting for her, and then she came down the stairs, looking as beautiful as ever. He would stand perfectly still, waiting, and then when she saw him she would cry out.

"Oh Drake, darling—but how is this?"

"Somebody else died, Sara, not me."

He closed his eyes to kiss her and felt her soft lips. Sara was one of those soft woman—the sweetest lips he had ever kissed.

"Hey, you asleep?" Nick bellowed in his ear.

"I can't come right away, Nick. I have an important engagement."

"What engagement?" Nick said indignantly. "What's more important than a contract?"

"Just this engagement," Drake said gaily. "But hold the contract, Nick. I'll get there sometime, today, tomorrow, one of these days."

He hung up and stood still, dreaming. He'd get there today, of course. When he and Sara had sat down on the sofa side by side, when he had kissed her again and again, when they had lunched together and told each other everything, he would glance at his watch and cry out.

"By gad, darling, I have an important engagement—I entirely forgot. You make me forget everything."

"A play, Drake?"

"Yes, *South Side of the Moon*, a new thing—it looks good."

"Come back soon." That is what she would say. "I'm so proud of you, Drake." That is what she would say.

"I'll come back," he would promise. "We'll dine together, shall we? We'll make our plans."

"I'll be waiting for you." That was what she would say, in her soft voice. It was softer than it used to be.

He bustled about the room, getting himself ready. He had one new shirt. He always kept one new shirt, just in case he might get an interview with a casting director. He began all over with another shower and a shave and then the new shirt and his better suit. He always kept one better suit. Then he hesitated. What about taking her something? He looked about the room at his few books, his small mementos, and then cried out aloud, snapping his thumb and finger, "Of course, the flowers!" He swept them all together, recovered a box he had thrown in the corner, packed them into it and tied the string carefully. Then he reached into his closet and took out a cane which he had not used for years, a slender bamboo cane tipped with imitation ivory which he had carried as the husband in the play. Pausing at the mirror he looked into it and saw someone he had not seen for a long time, a tall thin fellow whose pale face was alert and smiling, whose dark eyes were bright, a debonair sort of fellow, after all.

He smiled at the face, pleased at the resurrection. It was not bad, considering how dead he had been.

"Greetings," he said pleasantly to the face, and putting on his hat he tilted it slightly to one side and left the room.

Next Saturday
and Forever

ALL THROUGH THE WEEK she did not care for her looks, her hands or her hair. Only this one evening when she waited for Andrew did she feel that her fingers were too rough with sewing and that her dark hair was grey under her small brown hat. She had a second's thankfulness that since things were as they were, since they might not marry and live together, that she could wear her hat and so he need not see how heavy the grey was upon her head. There was a broad band of it over her forehead, sweeping down to the very ends of her hair and she was careful to keep her hands in her lap under the table.

It was a quarter past seven o'clock. That on a December evening meant black darkness. The little restaurant on Lexington Avenue was dimly lit. But she was glad for that, too. In the wry mirror opposite her the light felt kindly upon her face. She was still pretty in her soft way; there was still a childlike clearness in her brown eyes. When she was alone, when she woke in the morning and hurried to get the two rooms to rights and breakfast on the table for the children and her mother before she went to the dressmaker's shop where she worked, she was grieved to see how she looked. She was even sometimes sadly grateful that Andrew was not there to see her morning pallor and her dull eyes. Even Andrew, she thought, sitting here waiting for him, even Andrew might not love her at those times. Especially on the mornings when she knew that there must pass six whole days before she could see him again, her prettiness seemed gone from her. Then slowly as the days passed, day by day turning over like leaves on an empty calendar, days of rush, of sewing quickly all day long, of hurrying back to the children home from school and hungry, and to her fretful mother, slowly as the days passed she began to grow pretty again. For Saturday evening was coming, was near. At last it was come once more.

Then she gave the children their nickels to go to the movies with their grandmother; then when they were gone she bathed herself and dressed freshly from head to foot and dampened her hair and curled the ends around her ears; then she walked through the darkness if it were winter and through the twilight if it were summer and she met Andrew here at the restaurant. Sometimes he was before her; sometimes as tonight, she was first. It made no difference. It was harder for him to get away than for her. He had his petulant nagging wife to drag at him with questions and demands. She always knew how he was when he came in at the door. It would be any moment now. She glanced at the clock. Her heart stopped. It was agreed between them that if the other did not come in half an hour something had happened to prevent the meeting. She had waited twenty minutes.

Well, there were still ten minutes and she would not think what she would do if he did not come. Time enough to think of that when she was sure of the worst. Once when he did not come she had crept through the streets to the poor basement where he lived and had peeped in just to see him, if she could not speak to him. He was walking about with a child in his arms, a sick child. His wife was bent over the stove, frowsy, ill-tempered. The woman was talking and talking, and every now and then she flung up her head and screamed at one of the children, or at Andrew. She could not hear the words, but she could see the impatience, the movement of the jerked arm, the angry head. Every time Andrew passed the window he looked wildly out into the darkness, as if he knew her there. But he did not. She was crouched in the shadow, her heart aching to bursting. Ah, that had been a long week to wait!

Five minutes were gone, well, still she would not think what to do if he did not come. She looked about her. She would not think. She would look at the other people. Across the small room, against the wall sat two young things, a redheaded boy and a blonde girl. They were in love too. Strange how when you were in love yourself you knew it in everybody else! They were sitting side by side. Under the table their knees were pressed together and the toe of her little shoe rested on his foot. She could see it. The girl was adoring the boy, listening to him, her heart hanging on his every look. He was bragging boldly. Through the clatter of the restaurant she caught fragments of his boasts. "And then I caught him under the chin—like this, see? It was a cinch. He went over—like that! Gosh—now see what I've done!" He had made a large sweep with his hand and had overset his glass of water. The girl laughed aloud, adoring him. Her lips were framing words—it was easy to see what they were—"I love you—I love you—" The boy glanced about quickly and bent, pretending to mop up the water, and kissed her quickly.

The woman smiled to see it. She understood every movement, every look. There was nothing new in love, after all—it was all old and lovely and to be repeated over again and again. Its only newness lay in the new strength it brought wherever it came.

And then, just when she felt an intolerable pang of longing for Andrew and turned restlessly to the door, not daring to look at the clock, he came hurrying in, a slight dark tired-looking man, his black hair plainly white about his temples, and no hat to hide it.

He came to her instantly, as a bird to its home. They had so little time. They began at once, with no words wasted. They had to know at once that the other was there, was unchanged, and was warm and ardent and loving.

"Ruth—my darling!" he cried under his breath. "I wish you could see how you look! When I came in your face was turned to me like a rose. You're a rose, you know. You always make me think of a rose. When I remember what your life is, how you work—darling, darling, how can you keep your face like a rose, and your eyes such miracles for me?"

She looked into the wry mirror and laughed. She could see her face there under the brown hat, sweet and flushed and shining and very pretty. It was not at all the same face she would see tomorrow morning in the mirror. Yet this face was her own, her real face. They were themselves when they were together, instantly at ease.

He slipped into his seat beside her and she felt his thigh against hers, his knee against hers. She felt for his hand. Now they began their life together. They came here every week because once they had met here. Once she had been quite alone in the world, for what was the memory of Tom who had run away when Jimmie was born, and what ever were the three children whom she loved and faithfully served? She herself was quite alone, and so was he, married so sadly, and they sat here eating alone, one February night. Then she had looked at him and found him looking at her, and they began to love each other. Neither one of them could remember exactly how they began. It was five years ago, nearly, and the beginnings were dim. It seemed they had always met here like this and warmed each other like this.

She felt happy and excited and she longed to tell him everything at once. That was the way they both always felt the moment they met. They wanted to tell each other everything, the smallest things. First she must know how he really was. She held his hand under the table tenderly feeling it. It was warm and dry—not feverish? Sometimes he was a little feverish. But tonight not. She was relieved.

"Has she been—better?" she asked, tentatively.

"Well, she's been better than sometimes," he answered heartily. He nodded at the waitress and without a word she began setting before them their usual meal. "I had a hard time getting away because she wanted me to take her out. I just had to lie and say I had some work to finish at the office."

"Yes," she murmured.

They had discussed this matter of lies. They hated very much to lie, because they were both quite honest people. But of course there must be this one hour in the week, that is, if life were to go on at all. For the sake of them all it was better to have this one hour. They could keep on with their duty six days in the week if the seventh there was this hour.

"So I had her invite Mrs. Hicks next door, and they went off. Luckily for me Margie is big enough to take care of the little ones."

Then he must find out about her. "And you, my darling?"

"Just the same, Andrew—I'm always just the same," she answered, looking at him steadily.

He caught in his breath and held her hand hard. "I know it," he said, "that's what makes it possible for me to live at all. You're the lamp in my heart. If the lamp burns without failing, life goes on. If anything should happen to you—"

"Nothing will," she said, practically. She was determined to live as long as he did.

The food came on, soup in thick bowls, sausages, cabbage. They ate in silence for a moment, content in each other's presence. Once he laughed softly and said, "Look!" She followed his eyes and saw the boy and the girl teasing each other in an ecstasy of love, taking bites of food from each other's plates, sharing their shining and dangerous love.

"But they don't really know anything about it, do they?" she said quietly, smiling at him.

"Nothing!" he answered passionately. "How can they know love unless they've had the terrible loneliness you and I have had, until they have had our need of a refuge?"

The tears were suddenly in his eyes, and she took his hand again to still him. She said comfortably, "I like to think, when we eat together like this, that it's only one of three meals a day. I pretend we've had the other two meals and this is the last one before we go to our home and to sleep, never to part."

"It isn't right—what we're doing—" he said in agony. "It's not right. We're denying ourselves—"

"There, there," she said soothingly. "We've talked over all that, haven't we, dearest—over and over and over. We're not young and free. We have to keep on earning, don't we—between us there are seven little children to take care of—and two helpless women— they depend on us. We know we can't just think of ourselves. Don't let them spoil this little while." She glanced at the clock. "We have a whole hour—to sit here—to say it all over again—to tell each other *everything*."

But they did not talk much, after all. They sat, their hands touching, their shoulders pressed together, drawing in strength from each other. Across from them the two children finished their meal with red wine and laughter and shared a cigarette together. The restaurant was emptying, and now the boy bent boldly and kissed the girl, and every time he kissed her she laughed, and so he kissed her again to make her laugh again. The two older ones sat hand in hand and watched them, as they might watch children playing, and every now and then they looked at each other deeply and smiled. They did not need to kiss like that, they did not need to laugh. They drew their strength from some profounder passion, from some more intimate need than the need to kiss again and again. Once she asked, "Nothing new happened in the office?" "No," he said, "nothing will ever happen to me again except—this." She smiled for answer.

So the clock crept around again, and they saw it and looked at each other. At last she said gently, "We must go, beloved."

He held desperately to her hand. "I don't give up hope, Ruth," he said.

"No, indeed," she agreed cheerfully.

They waited a moment longer. It was always such rending of the flesh to move away from each other, to begin the seven days again. Sometimes, if everybody else were gone, they would kiss each other, too. But not always, and only if they were the last ones left. Something forbade their lightly kissing each other. There were still the boy and the girl. They could not kiss before those two gay children, playing at love—not one of their rare, almost painful kisses. They sat, waiting.

Then the boy tired a little. He was tired of making

love. His eyes wandered about the empty room. "Say," he said loudly, "let's go to a movie. I know a swell show."

He lifted the girl to her feet and the two sauntered out, hand in hand, careless, chattering, eager for something else.

Then they were the two left, the only two. It was hard to part, but they were able to do so. Besides, they were rested and made young again by being together. His dark face was less lined than it had been when he came in and in his eyes was peace. As for her, she knew by his worshipping gaze that she was beautiful. At this moment she was not weary, not sad, not lonely. She was beautiful and beloved. They loved and understood each other.

"Forever?" he said. It was the same every week.

"Forever," she said steadily.

They waited a moment, swept by the vastness of the solemn word. Then, since the room was empty except for a little waitress, yawning at a far table, he bent and kissed her gently on her lips. Once more they rose and went away.

The Lovers

GILES BREDON HESITATED at the corner of the street. From here he had always caught the first glimpse of his house when he had been away and was coming home again. It stood in the large square lawn, a solid old brick structure, the place where he was born, but it was no longer home. He had not seen it for more than a year, not since the day that he had packed his bags and left Lesley, his wife, standing in the living room, looking at him in silence. It was his last sight of her, and whenever he thought of her, he saw her as she had been at that moment, her dark eyes large and tragic, red stubborn mouth, ivory pale face against the soft straight black hair. She had said not a word when he stalked out of the room. At the threshold he had hesitated.

"Aren't you going to say anything?" he had demanded.

She shook her head and he had slammed out of the door.

Since then their communication had been through lawyers. Once a month he had paid the household bills and her personal allowance. When Judith, their only child, came to visit him in town at the apartment he was renting, he asked no questions concerning her mother, and Judith, chattering to him apparently about everything, never spoke her name. He had tried to make each visit interesting, notable for some amusement or person, hoping, as he recognized, half ruefully, that Judith would tell her mother that she had had a good time with him.

Then a week ago Colton Bates, his lawyer, had insisted on a meeting between what he called "the estranged pair." This meant simply that he, Giles, had to see his wife, Lesley, once more. At least he supposed that she was still his wife? At what moment did a man and woman cease to be husband and wife?

The day was fine, a warm wind blew from the south, and the flowering shrubs on every lawn proclaimed the spring. He was walking toward his house now. If the divorce went through he supposed the house would no longer be his. No, damn Lesley, that he could not bear. He would give the house to Judith, allowing her mother only the right to live in it. Lesley might be too proud to stay on such terms.

The trouble was that he and Lesley had married too young. He had been graduated from Harvard one day and married the next, like a fool! Their parents had not approved such romantic haste, but he and Lesley had been desperately in love. At that, he now wondered, how much of it had been real love? Both of them wanted to be independent of the formal old life in two formal old houses. Love had been confused with independence. He grinned sardonically at the thought.

"Why, Giles Bredon!" He was startled by a loud cheerful voice, and he looked across the pavement into a woman's face.

"Hello, Kit," he said.

It was Katharine Baker, a neighbor, and she was

down on her knees, planting something or other, as usual. George Baker, her husband, was a dull fellow, successful in the wholesale furniture business. Kit sat back on her heels and the sun shone down on her sunburned cheeks.

"Are you coming home again, Giles?"

"Only to talk lawyer business with Lesley," he said. Better to be frank and ruthless, else Kit would spread false good news over the whole neighborhood!

"Oh, Giles!" Her honest grey eyes were sad with reproach. "Lesley is so lovely—"

"There's nothing you can tell me about Lesley that I don't know," he said firmly.

"Giles, forgive me—there isn't anyone else, is there?" she pleaded.

"Nobody else for either of us," Giles said.

"Then what—"

"Then nothing," he said. "We have simply grown apart."

He smiled, tipped his hat and walked on. She would convey that speech everywhere. "My dear, I asked Giles myself and he said they had simply grown apart."

Well, it was the truth, so let it stand. He was at his own front door now. The place looked well kept, Lesley would see to that always. She was a good manager. The door stood open. She liked the cool fresh air, and he liked the warmth. Many a time he had shut this door.

Should he go in? It seemed absurd to ring the doorbell of his own house, but he rang it. He waited and no one came. The house was silent. He rang the bell again. Then he heard Lesley's voice calling from the upstairs hall.

"Please come in, Giles. I'll be down in a minute. Just go into the living room."

He went in, took off his hat and topcoat and put them in the closet under the stairs, then crossing the hall he entered the familiar place. He was shocked at the change. He had walked out of it a year ago, leaving it the big old-fashioned room that he had known since his earliest memory. What had Lesley done? The famous flowered wallpaper that his father had brought from Paris was gone. The walls were a strange white, an off-white that tinged on grey, the old dark green velvet hangings were changed to crisp yellow new ones, and instead of the brocades the furniture was covered with some rough material, the same strange white again. The long couch was cherry-red and so were two of the chairs. He sat down in another chair that he remembered as blue, which was now white, and felt aggrieved. Lesley had no right—

She came in, composed and fresh, looking exactly as usual. He stood up, confused. How does a man greet a woman who is his wife, or was, and still was, legally—should he kiss her? She settled it by coming to him and kissing him on the cheek lightly, almost carelessly.

"Well, Giles—"

She sat down in a cherry-red chair, and looked, he had to admit, very handsome in her black and white suit. No, handsome was too hard a word. She was beautiful.

"How are you, Lesley?" he asked.

"Very well, thank you," she said in her usual clear voice.

She was forty-four years old, he grumbled to himself and he felt that he looked ten years older than she was, after this year. Whereas she—but women were tough, he supposed. She didn't feel things the way he did. And, after all, she had the house and Judy, while he had lived alone in a damned apartment. He refused to remember for the moment that he had told himself often how much he enjoyed living in town alone.

"I suppose you have seen Colton Bates?" Lesley asked.

"He told me I'd better talk to you before we drew up the papers," he said.

And women were damned cold, he told himself. While he had been feeling sad, Lesley had been thinking about the lawyer.

"What grounds are you going to give for wanting a divorce?" he demanded belligerently.

Lesley opened her dark eyes at him. "I thought it was agreed—mental cruelty."

He had agreed, months ago, but now when he heard the words on her lips he instantly rebelled.

"Silly nonsense," he said. "It's the excuse people give when they haven't any excuse. You know there's been no mental cruelty."

"I don't know," she said. "It depends on what one means by cruelty. We were both cruel, perhaps. I mean—we weren't happy."

He agreed gloomily. "I don't know what was the matter with us."

"Nothing I did pleased you," she said.

"Nonsense," he said. He crossed and uncrossed his legs. "You criticized me for every little thing."

"Bicker-bicker," she said.

He scrutinized her face. Was she angry? No, she was curiously calm. Bicker-bicker was right. Their mutual irritation had pentrated into the depth of their relationship, destroying all unity.

They were silent. He perceived that she felt him looking at her and so she kept her eyes fixed on the window.

"It's cold in here," he said.

The moment he said the words he wished that he had not, although he had spoken thoughtlessly and not meaning in the least to recall the times that he had said exactly the same thing. She would retort, "I like the fresh air. You always want everything so hot."

But she did not. Instead, as though he were a guest, she rose and shut the front door and sat down again.

"The sunshine is warm," she said, "but there is a slight chill in the air."

He made an effort. "Well, it's mental cruelty then, is it?"

"Call it incompatibility, if you like," she said, "but that's rather old-fashioned, I believe. It's the same thing."

"It sounds silly to say people are incompatible when they have been married long enough to raise a child. In fact, the whole thing is pretty silly when it's put into words, except that—'' he trailed off, leaving the sentence unfinished.

"It is," she said reasonably, taking it up, "but it is also the fact that for some reason or other we are happier apart. Aren't you?"

"Aren't I what?" he asked, not listening. He kept staring at her. She was the woman he knew so well— and she wasn't. Just what—and why—was the difference? There was a charm about her that he had forgotten while they lived together. Now, seeing her after separation, he recognized it again.

"Happier without me," she said with a touch of old impatience. He had a habit of leaving sentences unfinished and not listening, and he remembered this guiltily.

"In some ways," he conceded, but not as happy, he felt, as he had thought he was. Now that he sat here, even though the room was strange, he felt a rush of old habit. The house, the life in it, his bedroom upstairs— and here—the way they used to spend Sunday mornings lounging around, newspaper all over the floor, break-fast when he felt like it, planning the spring garden—

"How is the tulip bed?" he asked. The tulips had been his pride, always blooming first before anybody's.

"They should be replanted next year," she said.

He leaned forward, forgetting. "Now, Lesley, they must be Holland bulbs. I'd better make out the list for you—"

She looked surprised. "Why, all right—but I

planned to be in Florida next winter, Giles. Judith goes to college in September and I'll be alone—unless you want the house? I'd rather like to move into town, I think—take an apartment, perhaps.''

He was suddenly angry. ''You'll find an apartment very cramped after a big house like this.''

''Then you take the house,'' she said stubbornly.

''See here, Lesley,'' he said, ''a man in a house is very different from a woman in a house. I have to be at my office all day.''

''Get a housekeeper,'' she said succinctly. ''That's about all I am now, anyway.''

''Oh, come,'' he protested. ''You are the mistress of a handsome establishment and you know it. Don't be sorry for yourself.''

What she might have retorted to this he did not know. He was ashamed of himself and was saved from proper punishment by Judith, running down the stairs and into the room between them, the wide skirt of her white dress flying out like wings behind her.

''Dad!'' she cried. ''Oh Dad, how swell to see you here!'' She enveloped him in soft bare arms. Soft? They were as strong as steel around his neck. She subsided on his lap and turned her face to her mother. Her eyes were bright blue, like his.

''Mother, have you told him?''

''We've been talking business,'' her mother said.

''You haven't told him!'' Judith cried.

''Told me what?'' he demanded.

She returned to him, clutching him again around the neck. He felt her fresh cheek against his lips.

"Dad, I'm in love!"

Against her cheek he mumbled. "Nonsense—"

"Not nonsense," she said, removing her cheek. "It's true—I'm in love—I'm in love—"

"Stop it," he said. "It sounds like a routine. Now tell me all about it."

His eyes met Lesley's, and he saw a secret smile in those dark depths.

"Love has hit Judith hard," she said. "It's the first time. Ah well!"

"Mother, don't be cynical," Judith commanded.

"You look such a child sitting there on your father's lap," Lesley retorted, amused.

Judith rose instantly, flounced her skirts and sat down in the other cherry-red chair.

"I haven't seen Dad for a week," she said furiously.

"I am not criticizing," her mother said mildly.

"You are," Judith cried in the same furious voice. Her cheeks, always cream pale, flushed pink and her blue eyes shone under a frown. "You're as cynical as you can be. You don't believe in love!"

"Come, come, Judy," Giles said. "You haven't even told me the fellow's name." He was rather enjoying the scene between his wife and his daughter. It brought him into the family again.

"It's only William Baker," Lesley said.

"Mother," Judith cried, "you know he wants to be called Bill! And how dare you say 'only'?"

"What—George and Kit's boy?" Giles asked, unbelieving. "Is he big enough to fall in love with? Last time I saw him he was still wearing—"

"Oh, shut up," Judith said and burst into tears.

Her parents looked at each other over her bent head and each caught remorse in the other's look.

"The first time is so hard," Lesley said in a feeling voice.

"Don't I remember," Giles said, gazing into her eyes. "I stopped eating and sleeping, and I camped under your window even after we had said good night twenty times or so."

Judith lifted her head. "Don't you dare compare Bill and me to you two! We're serious!"

Her face, still pink and white, was fierce.

"Darling," Lesley said. "We are only remembering. So will you some day."

"I won't," Judith said. "I shan't need to remember—I'll be living with Bill—and—and—our children—forever!"

Giles felt a sharp quickening about his heart. Anger? Pain? He did not know which.

"So we thought," he said.

His daughter flouted the idea. "Thought!" she echoed, scornfully. "Bill and I don't just think—we know!"

"Just what do you know?" Lesley asked. Her own cheeks were suddenly quite pink, and Giles, watching her, saw what he had never noticed before, that while Judith had his coloring, actually she looked like her mother. Lesley had been just such a fiery girl.

"You make me think of your mother, Judy," he said. "I remember a scene in this very room, as a matter of fact—not this furniture of course. Her parents and mine met here one evening to tell us that we were too young to be in love. God—there's a song about that now, isn't there, 'too young to love'! Well, they were right."

Judy stopped crying. She wiped her eyes, producing a small white handkerchief from inside her wide belt and mopping her face with it. "Maybe you and Mother were too young to love," she said. Her voice trembled. She was looking from one parent to the other. "Sometimes I think you'll never grow up. Bill and I are much older than you two in lots of ways. We were talking about it the other day. There's been so much to make us grow up—the war and—and everything the way it is now. We haven't loved in the easy way you did, thinking everything was going to be peaceful and happy ever after. We already know it isn't." She turned to her mother. "And that's what we know, Mother. And we know we can take it, if we're together, Bill and I."

Lesley lost her own temper, promptly concealing the fact as usual under icelike calm.

"You are being very childish without knowing it, Judith," she said. "You understand nothing about marriage. The qualities in Bill that you now think are wonderful will probably become—tiresome—as time goes on.''

''If they are,'' Judith said, ''nobody will know it. I'll stick to my bargain. I won't run out on him. I'll be too proud.''

A piercing whistle rose outside the open window. It hung in the air, a corkscrew of sound, prolonged and shrill.

''Is that Bill?'' Giles inquired.

He need not have asked. His daughter changed under his very eyes. Fury faded from her face, her eyes grew tender, her cheeks pale. She rose and floated out of the room, her full skirts swirling about her. She breathed out ecstasy and it hung in the air like a perfume.

He walked to the window, scarcely knowing that he did, and from there he saw the love scene, as old as humanity and new as today. A tall lean boy stepped over the side of a worn and winded-looking car, and striding up the walk, he met the girl at the door. There he took her in his arms. They kissed long and fervently, and Giles felt a queer faintness at the sight of his daughter's golden hair lying upon the shoulder of the boy's dark blue coat, and then remembered that this same faintness had attacked him about the heart when he and Lesley had first kissed so long ago.

''Have you told your folks?'' The boy lifted his head to ask the question.

''Yes,'' Judith said.

He could hear their voices clearly, as though they did not care whether they were heard.

"I told them," Judith said, not drawing away, her face still uplifted.

"What did they say?" Bill asked.

"Does it matter?" Judy asked.

They were gazing into each other's eyes.

"No," he said, and bent his head. Again they kissed.

This time, Giles told himself, he could not bear it. He stepped back, and stumbled against Lesley. She had tiptoed to the window behind him and over his shoulder had been watching the same scene.

"I'm sorry," he said, recovering himself.

"I'm not hurt," she said.

Each stepped back, too conscious of the moment's contact. They sat down, silent and listening, and Giles turned his head to the window.

"Isn't she going to bring him in?" he asked.

"I don't know," Lesley said. "She's so strange. She's cut herself off from us."

"We don't matter now," Giles said ruthlessly.

Lesley did not answer. Her hands were crossed on her lap, and she sat pensively looking at her rings.

"You are still wearing your wedding ring," he remembered irrelevantly.

"I thought I'd keep wearing it, if you don't mind," she replied. "It will save explanations, perhaps, when I'm travelling."

"As a matter of fact, you're still married," he said.

She flashed her dark eyes at him. "Are you trying to be cynical or helpful?"

He evaded this potential tinder. "They're getting in the car now," he said, looking at the window.

"Are they?" she said indifferently.

He was irritated. "See here, Lesley, we ought to do something—say something, at least, about this affair. After all, I didn't kiss you—like that—until we were regularly engaged."

"We were old-fashioned," she said in the same voice, indifferent and musing.

"They've changed their minds," he said, still watching. "They're coming in."

She did not reply and he lit a cigarette. Almost immediately they were at the door, the tall brown-haired boy, his thin face set and white. Not a handsome boy, Giles thought, much too tall and slender, but the army would fill him out. Of course marriage was absurd when there was the army ahead! By the time the boy got back Judith would be in love with someone else. If he had been separated from Lesley at the same age—

"Bill wants to talk with you, Dad," Judith announced from the door. Her voice was sharp, feminine, adult.

"Come in," Giles said. He held out his hand, and did not rise. "I wouldn't have known you, Bill—haven't seen you for a while, have I?"

"No, sir. I've been at college."

They shook hands. The boy's hand was bony but warm and firm.

"You've changed by several feet," Giles said, trying to be affable.

Bill grinned. "I've done some growing," he admitted.

"Hello, Bill," Lesley said in a low voice.

"Hello, Mrs. Bredon," Bill said. "It hasn't been many hours since two o'clock this morning."

"Very few," Lesley said.

Bill turned to Giles. "Judy and I were at a dance last night, sir. That's when we decided."

Giles felt paternalistic and despised himself and said nothing. Bill went on calmly, damnably calm, Giles thought, remembering his own sweating agony a generation ago in this very room, his parents sitting in these two chairs, now cherry-red, and Lesley's parents on the couch, her father wearing a formal cutaway and striped trousers because he was on his way to a directors' meeting at the bank, and her mother, he remembered, in a dove-grey dress of some sort. Lesley, sitting on the hassock by the window, had been in white the way Judith was now, and looking like an angel. He could remember how sick he felt with love that day, an actual nausea, a faintness in the breast, his voice weak when he wanted it strong, and he had sweated like a porpoise while she waited for him to defend her.

"I want you to know." His voice had actually squeaked, "Lesley and I are engaged."

"Really and truly engaged," she had echoed, almost in a whisper.

Bill was talking. Giles brought his reluctant mind back into the present.

"Judy needs security," Bill was saying, "and I can give it to her. We both believe in real love—lasting love, that is."

"Bill needs security, too," Judith put in. Her voice was still sharp, feminine, adult. "He has to go into the army. He's had his notice—twenty-one days. If we're married, he'll feel secure."

Lesley came out of her dreamy silence. "Marriage doesn't mean security—not any more."

"It's going to mean that in our case," Bill said definitely.

"This isn't just romance," Judith said with grimness. "It's love."

"Good God," Giles said. He lit another cigarette.

"Have you any objection, sir?" Bill said.

"Objection?" Giles repeated. "To what?"

"To me," Bill said.

"None in the least," Giles said. "After all, I've known you since you were born, practically, your family and so on. You're both too young, but I suppose you know that."

"I don't think being young has anything to do with it, sir," Bill said. "Not when you need security. You had it, sir, in your generation, I mean. I guess that's why you've thrown it overboard so easily."

Giles felt his collar suddenly tight. "What do you mean by that?" he demanded.

"It's a different world," Bill said. "Judy and I have to make our own security or there isn't any."

"We aren't complaining," Judith said. "We have to take it as we find it. But we don't want our children to—to go through what we have. We want them to be secure because we are."

Giles, listening to this speech, was about to say something scornful concerning young preachers when he saw his daughter's knees visibly trembling under her skirts. A child, after all, in spite of her being in love—his child!

"Who am I to tell you what to do?" he said suddenly. "Get married if you think it's what you want."

"Oh, go away," Lesley said under her breath. "Please go away, everybody!"

The girl and boy rose at once. Judith went to her mother and kissed her, then to her father, and kissed him. Then she caught Bill's hand and hand in hand they went to the door. There he turned.

"Goodbye, Mr. and Mrs. Bredon," he said.

Giles did not reply. He lit another cigarette and sat smoking it in silence. Lesley got up and moved about the room and sat down again. Outside the car snorted loudly and rattled away.

"Do you suppose they will run off and get married now, the fools?" Giles asked.

"Maybe they won't be as silly as we were," Lesley said. They remembered, silent and apart, that noontime scene in the tiny office of a justice of the peace. He remembered, too, the rush of freedom that swept him heavenward when they were pronounced man and wife. He had put his right arm about Lesley's shoulders and caught her with him out into the sunshine of that day.

"Nobody can part us now," he had said. "We are free and alone, man and wife!"

They had rattled off in an old jalopy of a car, too, something that he had put together himself, and had left behind when he went to college. But it had served their purpose until he had bought his first new car when they had been married a year.

"If they aren't as silly as we were, they'll be missing a lot," he muttered.

"Hadn't we better begin to talk business?" she asked.

He made an effort and felt himself entangled in a net of memory. That first night they had stayed in a country inn. He closed his eyes and leaned his head back. They had been absurdly ignorant, but brave with love. He had not thought of it in years.

"About this house," Lesley said. "I don't want it."

He opened his eyes and said harshly, "I certainly don't want it. What would I do with it—living alone?"

"Judith and Bill might be willing to live here with you," she suggested.

"I couldn't stand it," he retorted. "When we were

young it was only our parents who were self-righteous. Now it's the young people who are so damned self-righteous.''

She spoke with her first warmth. ''Aren't they! I assure you, it has been no easy task to live with Judith day in and day out. She had acted as though the collapse of the world were my individual doing. She and Bill, I suppose, will set it all right again. Maybe!''

''Maybe,'' he agreed. ''Anyway, it's their turn. Let them have the world. I'm sick of it.''

''So am I,'' she said heartily.

They were gazing at each other quite happily in unconscious agreement.

''I want to live with my own generation,'' he went on. ''Someone who knows what I'm talking about.''

''I feel the same way,'' she said.

His eyes fell on the cherry-red chairs.

''What in hell made you change this room?'' he demanded.

''I didn't want to,'' she said. ''It was Judy's idea.''

''You shouldn't have given in,'' he argued. ''After all, it isn't her house—not yet.''

''You had moved out,'' she reminded him.

''You told me to go,'' he reminded her in turn.

Reluctantly they smiled at each other, his smile grew into a grin, and she laughed.

''Oh dear,'' she said, wiping her eyes. ''I haven't had anything to laugh at for a long time.''

He crushed his cigarette and leaned forward, elbows on his knees. His voice was bold and bright.

"Why don't we run away again, the way we did before?"

She broke into waves of new laughter. "Oh, Giles, away from this same room—again?"

"Hideous, isn't it?" he said.

"Oh, I don't care," she said recklessly. "What's a house? Let Judy do what she likes with it."

"Let's make our own," he said ardently. He felt a new and sudden exhilaration, a fire in his heart again! "I've always wanted to build a house with extra bedrooms, lots of living room and terraces, and somewhere on a mountainside where we won't have to draw the curtains at night because there will be no one to look in."

"I've always hated this house," she confessed. "I hated it when your parents lived here, and I've hated it even more now that it's changed to suit Judy."

"Oh damn it," he said, "let's get away from them all!"

Insight, unusual and astonishing, illumined his face. He pounded the arms of his chair with his clenched fists. "Look here, Lesley—they're alike, these kids and their grandparents, both yelling for security. We know there isn't any, and we don't care!"

He crossed the room in three long strides and pulled her to her feet. "We've still got plenty of time," he said.

He swept her into his arms. Oh God, whoever said anything about young love? This was a thousand times better, to feel her back in his arms again, fitting him with all the experiences of the years. This, this was love!

"I can't live without you," he muttered, his cheek upon her hair.

"I've tried to live without you," she said in a small still voice, "it's too lonely."

"So now we know," he said.

The telephone rang, she tried to draw away and he held her fast. "Let's not have a telephone in our house."

"Let's not," she said.

But she flew to answer it. She listened, the receiver at her ear.

"Judy!" she whispered to him, and she told him the news, answering Judy, while she gazed at him.

"You're going to be married right away? Oh Judy—no wedding? We can't blame you, since we did exactly the same thing—didn't you know? Oh yes, we ran away and got married. What—you're going to live happy ever after, not like us? You may be surprised, Judy, very surprised! A week's honeymoon? Well, be happy, darling . . . Yes, he's still here."

She motioned to him and he came and took the receiver from her.

"Judy!" he shouted. "You ought to be ashamed of yourself! What have I done to get this treatment? Of course I'm angry! I haven't even given my consent— nobody asked for it! Well, it's up to you and Bill to make a go of it now, after all your boasting! What's that? Put him on, then!"

Bill's voice was at his ear. "I'm sorry we felt obliged to take things in our own hands, sir. We both felt we ought to tell you."

"Well, it's your responsibility. I wash my hands, etc!" He tried not to allow gaiety in his voice.

"I'll be responsible, sir," Bill said. His voice was serious, too serious.

"I don't need to tell you that Judy has a nice little temper of her own when she's crossed," Giles said with a touch of malice.

"I know," Bill said.

"Don't be too patient," Giles retorted. "And good luck!"

He hung up quickly and faced Lesley.

"We're free," he said.

"Free," she echoed.

They stood face to face for a moment, not touching. Slowly a smile crept up from their hearts and into their eyes to spread like sunshine over their lively faces. She stepped toward him and he took her in his arms, and in common accord, without a word, they began to dance. It was a medley of a dance, waltz and minuet and jive, he improvising, she following, embellishing while she yielded.

"Reckless," he murmured, "a reckless pair, and mad with love!"